May 7, 1987

Hey Pauline —

It's your Birthday —
isn't it great to
be 21 at last!

Love —
Diane

THE COLONEL'S DAUGHTER

AND OTHER STORIES

ROSE TREMAIN

Rose Tremain

SUMMIT BOOKS

NEW YORK

Copyright © 1983, 1984 by Rose Tremain
All rights reserved
including the right of reproduction
in whole or in part in any form
Published by SUMMIT BOOKS
A Division of Simon & Schuster, Inc.
Simon & Schuster Building
1230 Avenue of the Americas
New York, New York 10020
SUMMIT BOOKS and colophon are trademarks of Simon & Schuster, Inc.
This book was first published in 1983 in Great Britain by
Hamish Hamilton Limited
Manufactured in the United States of America

1   3   5   7   9   10   8   6   4   2

Library of Congress Cataloging in Publication Data
Tremain, Rose.
The colonel's daughter and other stories.
Contents: The colonel's daughter—Wedding night—
My wife is a white Russian—[etc.]
I. Title.
PR6070.R364C6   1984   823'.914   83-24316
ISBN 0-671-50463-0

Contents

The following stories appeared first in:

THE COLONEL'S DAUGHTER *Grand Street* (USA)
DINNER FOR ONE *Woman's Own*
MY WIFE IS A WHITE RUSSIAN *Granta*
A SHOOTING SEASON *Cosmopolitan*
CURRENT ACCOUNT *Woman's Own*
THE STATELY ROLLER COASTER *Encounter*

To Tony and Margery Parker
for their loyalty and love

The Colonel's Daughter

It is July. In Wengen, Colonel Browne is standing in the shallow end of the swimming pool of the Hotel Alpenrose, preparing himself for the moment of immersion on a late Friday afternoon. The sun, which has shone on the pool for most of the day, is grimacing now on the corner of the mountain. In moments, even before the Colonel has swum his slow and stately six lengths, the shadow of the mountain will fall splat across the water, will fall crash across the copy of *The Day of the Tortoise* by H. E. Bates that Lady Amelia Browne is peering at on her poolside chair. Lady Amelia Browne will look up from *The Day of the Tortoise* and call to Colonel Browne: 'The sun's gone in, Duffy!' The Colonel will hear her voice in the middle of his fifth length, but will make no reply. He will swim carefully on until he has made his final turn and his sixth length is bringing him in, bringing him back as life has always brought him in and brought him back to his wife Amelia holding his bath towel. Together, then, they will walk slowly into the Hotel Alpenrose, she with her book and the suncream for her white legs, he wrapped in the towel, shivering slightly so that his big belly feels cramped, carrying his airmail edition of the *Daily Telegraph* and his size ten leather sandals.

Ah, they will think, as they run a hot bath in their pink private bathroom and see their bedroom fill and fill with the coral light of the Swiss sky. 'Ah,' Amelia will sigh, as she takes the weak brandy and soda Duffy has made for her and lets herself subside onto her left-hand twin bed. 'Ah . . . ' the Colonel will bellow into his sponge, as his white whale of a body displaces the steaming bathwater, 'Cracking day, eh Amelia?'

*

At the very moment Colonel Browne finishes dinner, at the very moment Lady Amelia Browne smiles at him with fondness and remembers for no particular reason the war wound on his upper thigh which might have killed him but for a surgeon's skill, at this precise moment a green Citroen car enters the drive of one of the most beautiful houses in Buckinghamshire. On either side of the drive, great chestnut trees are in full candelburst. Multiple minute pink blossoms are squashed by the car as it comes on, fast, sidelights two glimmerings of yellow in the quiet grey dusk. No one sees the car. Garrod, the only person who might have seen it, had he been standing at the scullery window, might have heard it had be been walking the dog, Admiral, round the garden, doesn't hear it, doesn't see it because he is laid up with sciatica and dreaming a half-drugged dream of his days in the desert in his small sparse room at the top and back of the house. So the car comes on as if in silence, as if invisible, and stops soundlessly in front of the stone porch.

Out of the car gets Charlotte, carrying a suitcase – Friday visitor come from London as so many have come on summer evenings before, during and after the flowering of the magnolia on the south wall, getting out gratefully from their cars and smelling parkland, smelling cedar and chestnut blossom and aubretia and rock roses on the stones, then opening the heavy front door as Charlotte opens it now, standing on the polished scented parquet of the hall and thinking yes, this is how it always felt to be here: the portrait of the seventh Duke of Abercorn in momentous place at the foot of the staircase, luminous white face breathing a half-smile through the crust and dust of varnish and time; the stuffed blue marlin, caught by the Colonel near Mombasa, clamped fast to the wall above the massive fireplace, robbed of its body's dance and sheen – the trophies of lineage and leisure announcing to the tired Friday traveller that here, by a gracious permission only a few of us understand, is permanence, here at Sowby Manor beats one of England's last-remaining all-to-few unsullied hearts of oak. So welcome, if indeed you were invited. Garrod has lit a fire in the sitting room, drawn the curtains, turned down the beds. Come in.

Garrod sleeps. The dog, Admiral, older by human calculation than Garrod, barks feebly on his blanket-bed in the gunroom, gets up, turns a circle, sniffing his body warmth on the faded blanket and lies down again in the circle he has made. Charlotte stands by the Duke of Abercorn, above whom she has switched on a bar of light, hears the distant barking and sets her suitcase down. Charlotte is tall. The Duke of Abercorn stares mournfully through time at her bony shoulders and small breasts, at the grey of her eyes, pale-fringed with sandy lashes the colour of her hair that has been pulled back and up into an untidy bundle, making the face stark, a chiselled face, a whitewood face but with a line of mouth as thinly sensual as the Duke's own, a replica, it seems, more moist than his, merely pinker and half open now in expectation, in wonder at her own presence there in the hall, in the summernight dusk . . .

Move, says her voice, begin. So she, who like Saint Joan is obedient to her voices, begins to move out of the hall, opening a door to a dark pannelled corridor. She hears Admiral whimper. So lonely and quivering is the existence of this dog in the stone gunroom, she can imagine, as she carefully removes her shoes, its smooth wiry body tensed to the tiny sound she has made by opening the door and which floods its dog's brain with the obedient question: who?

Garrod sleeps. The dog sniffs the door, sniffs the dust on the stone in the minute dark space under the door. Charlotte walks barefoot down the corridor, remembering the dog's name is Admiral; on its expensive collar hangs a brass engraved disc: 'Admiral', Sowby Manor, Bucks. The stone flags are cold under her long feet. The house felt cold the moment she entered it. Now, outside, light seeps away, dusk becomes near-dark, the white roses on the wall are luminous. Charlotte opens the door to the gunroom and the dog springs up. The dog's feet reach almost to her breasts and she pushes it away, careful to fondle its head, to let it remember her, the Friday visitor who once came often to the Manor – long ago, before Garrod was hired, before Admiral grew old – and took the dog for walks in the beechwoods. 'Good boy Admiral, good boy . . .'

Still holding the dog's head against her leg, her hands calm, she reaches up into the gunrack, takes down the 12-bore cleaned so perfectly by Garrod since it last popped off the scattering birds in the valleys and woods of Sowby, on the heatherblown moors of Scotland, and places it on a ship's chest, this too cleaned and polished with Brasso by Garrod. She releases the head of the dog. It returns whimpering, nuzzling at her crotch and she pushes it away: 'Good boy, Admiral . . . ' The cartridge drawer is heavy. Charlotte takes out two cartridges only, drops them into the twin barrels, clicks the gun shut. Admiral barks suddenly. Charlotte's heart, so calm until this second, jolts under her skinny cotton sweater. She stares at the dog and at the gun. Dog-and-gun. She has seen them from childhood. Dog-and-gun and the red hands of the men going out into the frost: 'hurry, Charlotte, if you want a place in the landrover, if you want to watch the first drive . . .'

She closes the gunroom door, closes her thought of dog-and-gun. She slips silently back down the pannelled corridor to the hall, where the light is still on above the Duke of Abercorn. Garrod sleeps. She has never seen Garrod. 'I was before your time,' she might say, 'and, at the same time, long after it.' She knows the room, though. A man called Hughes slept there all through her childhood. He told stories of the war, stories of missions, crack units, lads with special training, heavily decorated lads, the ones who didn't die. Then Hughes died and somebody cocksure and young and unsatisfactory came and went with an Italian name and a pungent body odour, and then it was Garrod's turn, a meticulous man, she had been told, getting on, troubled by winter colds and sciatica, but thorough. And honest. You could leave the house in Garrod's care and be sure, on return, to find everything in its place, not so much as a sheet of writing paper missing from the bureau drawer.

Garrod sleeps. Charlotte, holding the gun, climbs the back stairs to his high landing. In the hall, near the Duke of Abercorn, the grandfather clock chimes ten. At this precise hour, in Wengen, Colonel and Lady Amelia Browne are served coffee – excellent Viennese coffee – in the comfy lounge of the Hotel Alpenrose, and the Colonel, nodding at the waitress, reaches for his cigar case. In Garrod's dream, he is lying on a stone. The sky is empty and yellowish white with colossal heat. He tries to move the stone from under him, but the stone is grafted to the small of his back. Charlotte reaches his door. She listens. She can't hear the agony of his dreams. She hears only her own breaths, like sighed warnings, turn back, leave the gun by the front door, go out into the dark and fly. Garrod wakes to night-time and sciatica pains. He turns over, grumbling, tucks his head into the pillow. Sleeps. The door opens. Out of darkness and sleep come the command, the drumroll, the moment when, from nowhere, the wild animal leaps: 'Get up, Garrod!'

*

At ten o'clock on this warm night, scriptwriter Franklin Doyle, born Colorado, USA, 1936, is scratching his chin, trying to save a love affair and failing. Opposite him, across a white table in his rented London flat, a woman called Margaret, sullenly, whitely beautiful, is spilling guilt-corroded truths about her body's longings for a man called Michael that squeeze and bruise the chest of Franklin Doyle so that he has to gulp for air and begin this repetitive scratching of his face to keep himself from laying his greying head on the table and wailing.

'It wasn't,' says Margaret, 'the kind of thing I wanted to happen. I didn't invite it.'

'Yes, you did,' says Doyle pathetically, 'at Ilona's party you sat at the creep's feet.'

'There weren't any chairs. Ilona never provides chairs.'

'He was sitting on a chair.'

'On a sofa.'

'On a fucking sofa. Who cares? You sat and fawned and I brought you drinks. But you know you've gone mad, don't you? You know he'll leave you, don't you?'

'He says he loves me, Franklin.'

'And you believe the asshole?'

'You don't need to call him that.'

'Yes, I *need*. For me! Have you forgotten about *me*? You're screwing my life up – and yours – for an asshole!'

'I told you, I didn't want this to happen . . .'

'Why don't you go, Margaret?'

'What?'

'Now. Just go now.'

Margaret is silent, frightened. She's used to Franklin Doyle, his flat, his fruit press, his lumpy dressing gown, his electric typewriter.

5

'Why now?'

Doyle puts his hands round his head and scrapes his scalp. 'For my sake.'

Margaret feels homeless, adrift, afraid of night-time and cold weather and dreams.

'Can't I go tomorrow, Franklin, when I've had time to fix something up and pack . . .?'

'I'll pack for you,' says Doyle, throwing his body up and out of the heavy designer-designed chair, hurtling it breathlessly towards his bedroom where his clothes and Margaret's, thrown together, softly litter it. He picks up at random a brown bra, a pair of high-heeled sandals, a pink sweater, a copy of *Ten Days that Shook the World* (a gift from him, unread), a jewellery box and a white nightdress and throws them into a pile on the double bed. He drags a suitcase from the top of a louvered wardrobe and begins tossing things in, scrunching and crumpling them, magazines, boots, tights, shirts, scarves, Tampax, leotards, dresses . . .

Margaret, relieved of her confession, alive to the sudden consequence of that confession, starts to sob for what she has destroyed, starts to weep and weep as her possessions go tumbling in. She feels vandalised, spoiled.

'I've nowhere to go!' she says. Doyle stops snatching her belongings, slams the suitcase lid on the stuff he has collected, zips it up and hurls it at her. 'Go to the creep! Go and bawl in his lap!'

So Margaret gathers up the case, remembering item by item all the things she is leaving behind, takes her pale jacket from a peg in the hall, turns, stares at Doyle, at his clenched hands, at his mouth, opens the door of the flat, turns again, sees Doyle through her shimmer of tears, goes out onto the landing lit by a brass chandelier and closes the door behind her. Slowly, and with sorrow she never expected, she walks down the stairs.

Doyle is at the sitting-room window. He pushes back the net curtains which smell mustily of dust and city rain, waits for the sound of the front door and the white figure of Margaret creeping out with her suitcase into the London night. He feels the failure and rage of forty-seven years lift his arm and bring it crashing down onto the window. Margaret slips from view. A cascade of glass fragments hurtles two storeys onto the pavement, startling a middle-aged Bavarian sculptress walking her dachshund on a tartan lead. '*Mein Gott!*' she exclaims and gazes up. She sees the light at Doyle's window. Nothing else. She walks on.

*

Near dawn, which comes early on their side of the mountain, Colonel Browne half wakes and mumbles across the space between him and his wife in her twin bed: 'Funny old Admiral didn't get his share of the meat.'

Lady Amelia sits up and stares at her husband's arm which is dangling onto the carpet. 'Duffy?' she says, 'What's this about meat?'

Colonel Browne opens a yellowed eye, notices his trailing arm and withdraws it into the safety of the Swiss-laundered duvet.

'Alright Amelia?' he asks.

She has put on her bedjacket.

'I was perfectly alright until you woke me up with some nonsense about Admiral and meat.'

'Meat?' The Colonel strokes a few strands of hair into place across his head. 'Got that damned pins and needles in my hand again. Must be the birds.'

'*Birds?*'

'Vultures or something. Dream, I suppose. Must've been. You put a carcass out on the lawn and all these birds came...'

'This is a holiday, Duffy dear,' says Amelia gently but firmly, 'No nightmares on holiday.'

*

Yet at dawn, in his Camden basement, Jim Reese is dreaming his habitual nightmare which no holiday has ever obliterated since he was a Brighton schoolboy and his mother's house stank of lodgers' tobacco and frying eggs. He dreams and redreams the day his room is given away to Mr John Ripley, a North Lancashire toys and novelties rep making a summer killing on the south coast, and his boy's bed is squashed into a suffocating space no bigger nor better than a cupboard, and all his *Eagle* cutouts are torn down and his drawer of fag cards emptied for Mr Ripley to lay his handkerchiefs and his metal hip flask in.

7

Jim Reese wakes and stares out at pale light on the area steps. He is sweaty, uncomfortable, suffocated by the dream. All his life, since the Brighton days, he has moved on – place to place, woman to woman – and yet he has always felt contained, fenced up. John Ripley's ghost and the ghost of his mother frying eggs have gawped at his efforts to understand himself. Now he feels emptied of understanding. Emptied of the will to understand. He has a set of drums. Playing these, he feels intelligent. He soars. He knows life is for living, learning, creating. He wanted to form a band or group. He knew a singer, Keith, getting small-fry gigs but confident, with a cracked black-sounding voice like the voice of Joe Cocker. Keith was interested in the group idea for a while, till he got a US recording contract and pissed off into the big time. Now Keith sings in Vegas and Jim Reese is where he is, looking out at the area wall. The drums are silent most days. Sometimes he polishes the chrome and wood, because if things get tougher than they are, he might be forced, just to hold himself together, to sell them. Two weaknesses have blighted his life and he knows them: he cannot sell himself and he cannot get angry. It isn't that he doesn't *feel* rage. He feels it alright, souring his blood, a poison. Yet he can't express it, just as he can't express himself (only through his hands on the drums). Like his person and his will, his anger is contained, walled up, silent.

Jim Reese gets up, lights a cigarette, looks at his watch. He can hear a blackbird in the cherry trees above his window. He begins listening for a car. He returns to the bed and sits on it, still smoking, still listening. High summer, yet his body is pale – kept underneath the road where soon trucks will thunder, kept uselessly out of sight. He is thirty-seven. Far too old, says his mother's fat-spattered ghost, to be a pop star. You should have put all that out of your mind.

Time passes. He makes tea, sits and waits. Sun glints on the rail of the rusty area steps. Saturday traffic starts to rumble. He feels knotted, anxious. Charlotte. He says her name, listens to the minute echo of her name that hangs for a second in the drab room. When she is with him, he feels breathless, hot. Her intelligence suffocates him. Now, without her, he feels the same breathlessness in his fear that she's deserted him, as he's sometimes wondered if, even hoped that, she would. Yet the flat is hers and everything in it except him and his drums. In place on the desk is her typewriter and in place beside it, half finished, is her latest article, *Eve and the Weapons of Eden*. She worked on the paper all the previous day, he remembers, until seven-thirty when she came and found him sitting by the drums with a tin of chrome-cleaner and a T-shirt rag, crouched on the floor beside him and told him: 'I'll be out most of the night. I'm driving to Buckinghamshire, to collect some things. I can't say what they are. I'll show you when I get back – probably very late, towards morning.' He took up the chrome-cleaner and the rag blotchy with stain and didn't look at her as she went out, carrying a suitcase. I don't own you, he said to her when she could no longer hear him, don't imagine it.

The tea is cold. The traffic is loud. The traffic reveals to him, day after day, his own stasis. His air is blasted with the lead fumes of other people's purpose; they fart their travelling ambitions into his face. He thinks of moving, as he has always moved, on. Somewhere quieter. Wales, even. Go to a mountain and hear the silly bla of sheep. Why not? Quit the notion that you can ever make anything of the city, or the city of you. Yet it is Charlotte who holds him, balanced on the edge of being there and not being there. She stands between him and his own disappearance. She feeds him tiny grains of her own purpose in the meals she makes and a little of herself creeps inside him.

Jim Reese will wait for another twenty-seven minutes before the green Citroen is parked near the gate to the basement and he sees Charlotte come slowly down the iron steps. In these twenty-seven minutes, a brilliant yellow sun rises on Wengen, flooding the balcony of Colonel and Lady Amelia Browne's room in the Hotel Alpenrose. Lady Amelia, wearing a blue robe de chambre, slips out onto the balcony without waking the Colonel, who has returned to his muddled dreaming, and begins her breathing exercises, gasping in the champagne air, dizzying herself with the cutting breath of the mountain. Into her mind, as her thin chest rises and falls, comes a delicious flowering of appreciation for the well-ordered world spread out like a gracefully laid table before her. Even, she notices, the arrangement of geraniums on the balcony itself is scrupulously wise, colours tossed into each other, growing, spreading, hanging, each bloom excellently placed. For Amelia Browne, order in all things has been an absolutely satisfying principle of

9

sixty-eight years. In her valuable Victorian dolls' house, given
to her when she was four, the little pipe-cleaner men and
women she moved from room to room never – as occurred in
the dolls' houses of her friends – stood on the beds nor lay
down on the kitchen floor.

Charlotte is lying on the basement bed. The traffic is roaring
now. Jim Reese finds her beautiful in the early morning light,
with her tired eyes. He touches her with a tenderness he often
feels yet can seldom express.

'Jim,' she says, pushing away his hand, 'this is the most
important day of my life.'

Jim leaves her body, snatches up the cigarette packet. He
stares at the crammed suitcase she has planted in the middle of
the room. The explanation, he thinks suddenly, will be worse
than what she has done. Because she is grave with achievement. She sits up, pushes wisps of hair out of her eyes.

'Open the suitcase,' she says.

Jim feels cross, weary. Revelations have always disturbed
and irritated him. But Charlotte's eyes are pools of red. It's
as if she's tracked for days and nights across some desert,
living only on her will. Her hand shakes as she fingers her
hair.

'Go on . . . '

Bored, resigned, he goes to the suitcase and opens it. As the
lid springs back and the case falls with a thud onto his bare
feet, bruising them with its extraordinary weight, Jim curses,
tips the case, extracts his feet, kneels and rubs them.

Now he looks into the case for the first time and is motionless. Charlotte's red eyes stare at his crouching back and over
his shoulder.

'Jesus Christ!'

'It's for you. Some of it for my work. But most of it for you.
There are other things in the car – pictures and a clock . . . '

So he begins to scoop it all out now and pile it round himself:
loops of pearls, diamonds stiffly jointed into necklaces and
bracelets and inset with emeralds, gold chokers and chains and
pendants, a moonstone tiara, rings, earrings, jewelled paperweights and boxes, boxes of amber and onyx and lapis lasuli,
an ivory fan, silver knives, forks, spoons, silver tea spoons and
napkin rings and salt cellars, silver table birds, bronze statuettes of deer and dogs and naked women with fishes, gold snuff

boxes and cigarette boxes, tortoiseshell card cases and combs and brushes . . .

So he is trapped, between this weight of devastating objects at his feet and Charlotte's burning at his back.

'We'll put you on the road now. Pay agents. Find someone to replace Keith . . . '

He looks dumbly down, stirs the treasures and they clink and clack. Minute lasers of light glance off the diamonds. 'Shit,' he says.

Charlotte stands up, crosses to him, crouches down.

'Jim, it's a simple conversion.'

Conversion? When he couldn't understand her, he hated her.

'It's so obvious, so right. We convert all this artifice into life.'

'Shit,' he says again.

'It's the most perfect thing I've done.'

But Jim stands up, kicks a pearl necklace away from him like a snake and it scudders under a chest of drawers. He can't look at Charlotte with her eyes like coal, so he turns away and leans his head against the wall. I want to break her, he thinks now. I want to break her for imagining this. For her vanity. She relegates me, miniaturises me: 'his life is so pitifully small, it can be transformed, reshaped by the selling of pearls and little boxes and ornaments.' But yes, for once in my life, I want to break someone. I can feel it start. Anger. Starts in my temple, but pushes out across my shoulders and down all the length of my arms and into my hands.

'I could kill you!'

His voice is a sob, weak, vanquished. But when he senses her moving to him, he is round like a whip and facing her. She reaches out to him, but he binds her arms to her side and shakes her, shakes her till she screams and pulls away, stumbles over the suitcase and almost falls. But no, he grabs her again and his hands cut deep into her arms, so hard does he grip, because he can feel her strength, equal to his and he must keep hold, keep hold and let it mount in him, the new anger so long buried in bone marrow and trapped, but now flooding muscle and sinew, pushing and bursting till it hurtles from him and he sees it arc and fall in Charlotte's body hurtling over into the air, then falling, falling as slowly as his long cry, her head crunching the grey metal of the typewriter and all her papers crushed and scattered as the body dives to the floor and is still.

Jim Reese gazes at the ribbon of blood threading her golden hair. And breathes.

*

A blue ambulance light turns. Four thousand miles from the ancient, restless mother he is dreaming of, Franklin Doyle is driven to hospital covered with a red blanket. All night, blood from his flayed arm flowed onto the vinyl floor of his kitchen, where he had stumbled in search of cloths with which to bind it, and where, as he began to wrap it round with a faded jubilee tea towel, a deep unconsciousness tipped him head-first into violent and useless dreaming. He lay with his head in the cat litter tray. The cat (a London stray who lent permanence to his long sojourn in the city) came and sniffed at his nostrils, sniffed at his blood, put a probing paw into it, licked the paw, then went to her milk saucer and drank, leaving a fleck of blood in the little saucer of milk. She urinated feebly near to Doyle's hair, then wandered to the sitting room, where she went to sleep on the sofa. Mrs Annipavroni, who made a tiny income cleaning the homes of exiles like herself, found Doyle at eight-thirty and rang for an ambulance. By that time, he was near to death. This would be the first time in Mrs Annipavroni's life that she could claim to have saved a life – unless you included her children, whose lives she saved in her mind many times a day.

As Doyle is received by the hospital, sunlight falls into the gunroom, where the dog, Admiral, has begun a violent barking and tearing of the door, a yowling and whimpering which express its desolate confusion. Its bladder is full. It is yowling for the damp and earth and shiny leaves of the rose beds, yowling for Garrod, jailor and deliverer.

Garrod is lying in the hall. The yellow bar of light over the Duke of Abercorn's portrait is still on, though the sun is flooding in and glimmering on the dead scales of the stuffed marlin and the post has crashed into the wire basket fitted to the inside of the letter box. It is at this moment when, if Colonel Browne were at Sowby Manor, he would be relishing a substantial breakfast and Lady Amelia toying with an insubstantial one. Then they would separate, he to his study to write letters and orders concerning the estate, she to hers, where she would spend considerable time rearranging her snuffbox collection before settling down at her bureau to 'tidy up a few odds and ends'. But the thoughts of Colonel and Lady Amelia Browne are not with Sowby. They are certainly not with Garrod, lying under the light of the Duke of Abercorn in the thick pyjamas he's had for eleven years. Their thoughts are with the Swiss morning that has broken so exquisitely, with such purity of light, on the thirteenth day of their holiday.

'Lunch at that nice high-up place with the fat owner?' says the Colonel as he dresses.

'The Glochenspiel?'

'That's it. Fancy that, do you?'

Lady Amelia has put on a lilac dress and new lilac shoes. She feels weightless, young.

'So pretty, the Glochenspiel.'

'Cold lunch at the Tannenbaum, if you prefer?'

'No, no. The Glochenspiel would be lovely, Duffy. What a heavenly day!'

So they go out – the large man and the thin, meagre-breasted woman – into the 'heavenly day', while Admiral pees in zigzags onto the gunroom floor and Garrod's doleful breaths confirm the pattern of his life: through seventy years he has rendered service and found none in return.

*

But Mrs Annipavroni and Jim Reese are doing the ultimate service – saving lives. Charlotte's head is bound so thickly the brilliant hair is hidden to all but Jim who mourns it, knowing it will be shaved when the head is stitched. Like Doyle, Charlotte rides to hospital under a red blanket. Like Doyle's dreams, hers are of her mother. And it is through the same hospital doors that Doyle has been wheeled only moments ago that Charlotte now travels, along the same corridor, nurses pushing, hastening, flat, bright light tingeing her palor with green, Jim Reese, a frayed tweed jacket put on over the vest he has slept in, jogging and pushing with the nurses till green swing doors open and receive Charlotte on the trolley and close on Jim, while a surgeon holds his hands up for the sterile gloves, moistens his mouth before the mask is tied round it. Jim stares at the closed doors. Only then, as Charlotte is snatched from him, does he remember the diamonds, the silver spoons, the gold and onyx boxes that still littered the floor when the ambulance men arrived to take her away.

*

Just before mid-day on this Saturday which is warm in the Swiss Alps, warm in Buckinghamshire and stickily hot in London, the police arrive at Charlotte's flat. The door is unlocked and they walk in: Sergeant McCluskie and Police Constable Richards. A voice growls on McCluskie's intercom. He snatches it and speaks quietly to it, like a man calming a dog: 'Delta Romeo X-Ray two five McCluskie. Arrived Flat Nine, Five Zero Ballantine Road. Er. Valuables. Liberal quantity of. Pictures and gun in Citroen car. No sign of residents, over.'

By 12.10, Charlotte's hoard has been returned to the suitcase which is wrapped in a polythene sack like a corpse and placed with the gun and the paintings in the boot of McCluskie's Granada. Delivering the treasure into the surprised hands of Camden Police HQ, McCluskie is then ordered to find Jim Reese and bring him in for questioning. McCluskie sends PC Richards to buy him a cheese sandwich from Vincente's Sandwich Shop. Vincente Fallaci is a cousin by marriage of Mrs Annipavroni, who has recently saved the life of Franklin Doyle. But such is the fine mesh of the British judicial system that this extraordinary fact entirely escapes it, and the relatedness of Julietta Annipavroni and Vincente Fallaci swims away from detection like a tiny glimmering sardine.

McCluskie and Richards drive to the hospital. Charlotte Browne is in no danger, they are told. However, the head wound is more than superficial. She is weak. She is sleeping. She cannot talk to them, and no, Mr Reese, who accompanied her in the ambulance, has not returned. Nobody can remember seeing him leave, yet he isn't there. McCluskie says he will wait and parks his heavy, muscular body on a plastic chair which creaks under his buttocks. Richards is ordered back to 50 Ballantine Road, to 'clobber' Jim Reese if and when he returns there. Meanwhile, police at Camden are sifting the diamonds, the lapis lasuli boxes, the bronze statuettes of naked women with fishes and trying to trace their origin. Meanwhile, Charlotte and Garrod and Doyle lie in pools of light and dream of their loneliness.

It's lonely, lonely utters Charlotte child to her parents on a sand-dune, to be sliced as I have been sliced with Timothy Storey's metal spade, lonely, lonely to feel the blood of my buried leg flow into the sand as Timothy Storey runs away to his Nanny in a deck chair. I call out – to you, to Timothy Storey's Nanny with her crochet, to anyone – but no one comes to the bleeding leg in its tunnel of sand, no one comes because I am no longer here, I have slithered away in my own blood and the same tide that washes away the crochet pattern inadvertently dropped by Timothy Storey's Nanny will wash away the shiny crimson puddle that was once a girl, only child of a Colonel, a girl with hair the colour of the sand which now receives her life.

Far away on the dunes, the wind clutters through the pages of Colonel Browne's *Daily Telegraph,* slaps through Lady Amelia's copy of *The Day of the Tortoise* which she is reading for the first time. Above and below and round and inside the wind, all is silence.

Garrod has turned. He lies face up to the sun. The stone in his back has turned and grown in size and weight and sits on his white chest. Heat floods his head. His head drips with the pain of the boulder flattening his heart inside the light and brittle rib casing. His heart has become a moth, beating its wings in a glass bottle. Far away where the tanks are massing, where the lads cool their skulls on their ice-blue visions of Rommel's eyes, a dog called Admiral is yowling for the battles to come, and the dead.

In slatted light, blood drips and fills, drips and fills. The body of Franklin Doyle is returning, drip by drip, from the death gathered up in the wide arms of Julietta Annipavroni and exchanged by this exile for an exile's life. Doyle is enjoying his journey back to existence. The way is littered with hope. This hope takes the form of glittering stones and flints as dazzling as jewels. He picks his way among their sharp surfaces, treading softly, walking on, on to the beat of a muddled verse twanged out by an old man whose skin has the colour and texture of rust:

> 'Fuck the Lord and screw damnation,
> Pappy's bought a gasoline station!'

Only the hand holding his is missing, the quiet hand of a girl called Margaret with shiny eyes and a fawn summer coat. She is hiding somewhere. She refuses to come out and introduce herself to the rusty man, his father, singing his rhyme. She is waiting, out of sight. Why waiting? Doyle doesn't know. But he walks on. Happy.

*

Colonel Browne leads his wife onto the cool terrace of the popular mountain restaurant, the Glochenspiel.

'It's so perfect,' sighs Amelia, 'don't you think?'

All, *all* that day is singing and yodelling with joy in the heart of Amelia Browne.

'They know how to do things up here,' smiles the Colonel.

Down below, in the basement of number fifty Ballantine Road, Constable Richards, alias Delta Romeo X-Ray two four Richards, picks up scattered papers, some torn, some stained with blood, and begins to read an article entitled *Eve and the Weapons of Eden* by Charlotte Browne. Constable Richards's A-level results enable him to understand that the article is talking to him about the oppression of women and their children, born and unborn, by the militaristic souls of the descendants of Adam. Constable Richards takes out a slice of Dentyne from his heavy blue pocket and chews on this anxiously, perplexed as he follows the jumpy words, the capital letters of which keep leaping up above the line, but which begin to reveal to him patterns, looping, diving, zigzagging, the mighty capitals standing over them like irregular trees, patterns of thought for which his A-levels, his obligatory studies of Marx and Mao, his months at the Police Academy have not satisfactorily prepared him. Into the hands of women, say these orchards of words, we commend the salvation of mankind. Constable Richards bites on the Dentyne, sighs, sets the papers down, rubs his eyes.

'Frightening muck!' he whispers to himself. But one sentence lurks in his mind. He has arranged this sentence into a rectangle which looks roughly like a door with no handle:

Our movement, like our sister movements of the eighteenth and nineteenth centuries, is hobbled not only by public apathy and public pig-ignorance but also by lack of money.

For several minutes he stares at the door, drawing and re-drawing its lines in his head. Then he picks up the receiver of a green telephone that sits on Charlotte's desk near to her typewriter and makes an important call to Camden HQ. Detective Inspector Pitt, CID, a smart, quiet stick of a man, offers Richards his curt congratulations.

*

And a clean blond waiter arrives. His hand is golden in the tableau of white cloth, crystal glass and green wine bottle that settles picturesquely into Amelia's mind. Beyond the high terrace, the sun is very hot. Blue butterflies flutter above a bank of euphorbia blooms.

'I think,' says Amelia, 'that these mountains simply must have been the original Garden of Eden. Don't you, Duffy darling?'

*

Jim Reese is on the move. As the train hurtles towards Brighton, he makes a simple plan for the recovery of himself. *Easy.* Everything's easy when you take control and stop the other fuckers shaping your life. Especially women. First his mother: 'I know you'll understand, Jimmy, I need the money and our Mr Ripley's a *very* good resident, so I see no alternative, now that it's a question of a long stay, to giving him your room . . . ' Then, years later, Charlotte: conning him he could be something because of a caseful of stolen glittery shittery richness. The gall. The temerity! The dumb insensitivity! Jim Reese pummels the armrest of the British Rail seat. Strong women. How he has come to fear the smell and flesh and the souls of strong women. Never again will any woman matter to him. They will simply *be* matter: thighs, breasts, cunt. Dispensible. Uncherished. Sheer matter. And yet, perhaps not even that . . .

'Ticket!' snaps the train guard. Jim Reese returns to the stuffy carriage and the fleeting summer fields outside it. As he hands the guard his ticket for clipping, he decides that on arrival he will go straight to the beach.

It is late afternoon when he arrives. Families with rugs and towels and windbreaks on the pebbly sand are kindly lit by the deepening sun. Children make a bobbing and jumping line to the ice-cream van with its little jangle of Italian music. Posters advertise a costume exhibition from some TV Classic Series at the Pavillion. From the stately white houses at the east end of the front, dogs are harnessed for teatime walks by retired people in baggy clothes. Brighton. Jim stares. The sea rolls in, majestic but calm. He fills his lungs and begins to walk towards it.

*

The sunlight is slipping from the hall at Sowby Manor when Garrod leaves Rommel's desert at last, leaves his old comrades with their ice-cold visions of German eyes and wakes in the light of the Duke of Abercorn. He is lying with his head on the first stair. Inside his pyjamas, the pain is lessened. Slowly, tremblingly, he pulls a shaky old hand from under him and lets it knead his chest, exploring for pain and stones and weights. Under his hand, now, is his mothflutter of a heartbeat, irregular and thin. His hand sends no message of reassurance, only of confusion. His head lolls on the stair. Inside his head is, far away, the crying of an animal. He stares up. The Duke of Abercorn gazes above his head, out towards the fanlight of the front door and the tender sky beyond.

Garrod sucks his lips, removes his hand from his chest and presses it, palm down, to the cold wood floor. He pushes with this hand and arm till all the top half of his body is raised and leaning on the stair. His body feels empty and cavernous and dark. His heart flaps feebly like a bat inside this cave of flesh. He listens – to his heart, to the dog's yowling. He knows, yet cannot remember why he is alone in the house. Only the dog, perhaps, is in it somewhere, in a room too far away to find. The grandfather clock chimes six.

'M'lady,' he mumbles. Yet he knows she isn't there. He is merely inviting this cool, once beautiful woman to save him from the desert of his dreams. And there it is, about to form around him again: the terrible sun, the tanks like insects, a circling bird, higher than unimaginable height. So he fights it. He clings to the banister, holds fast to the shape and feel of the banister. The desert blurs, recedes, Garrod is panting, drenched with effort. Yet the banister is there, solid, real, a lighthouse, a mast . . . And the lifeboat is coming closer, closer. Onto the gravel of the drive bounds Detective Inspector Pitt's white Rover. Beside him, held tightly to herself by her inertia reel seatbelt is WPC Verna Willis.

'Beautiful house, Sir,' ventures WPC Willis.

'Yes,' snaps the dry Pitt.

And they come on.

*

Doyle is stitched, bandaged, replenished. He wakes and stares at the bottle of blood sending its drip drip of life into his arm. He does not yet know that Julietta Annipavroni saved his life, yet senses that hours ago, in a featureless darkness, it may have needed saving.

He is grateful. A young nurse is bending over him and he takes her smile into his head.

'Okay, Mr Doyle?'

The nurse has a fine, thin mouth and an olive complexion. She might belong rightfully to India or even to Italy. Doyle cannot yet say.

'My oh my!' he says. His mouth feels parched, like an old man's mouth. The nurse lifts him with ease, holds a drinking cup to his mouth. He sucks water, his head nudging the nurse's breast. He lies back on his pillow and tries a smile. The smile cracks him. He feels the need to apologise.

'Did I say anything about a gas station?' he asks.

The nurse smooths his sheet. Her arm is covered with a fluff of dark hairs.

'I didn't hear it.'

'Had a hell of a dream – 'bout my Dad. He died in '63.'

'I'm sorry.'

'Did I miss a day or anything?'

'Sorry?'

'What day is this?'

'Saturday.' And she examines the watch pinned to her starched apron. 'Six ten in the evening.'

It is then that Doyle remembers Margaret. Margaret is miles away on the other side of London, snoozing with her new lover, Michael, in her new lover's new double bed. These bodies are hot and gentle and drowsy, but down the corridor from the room in which Doyle has just woken is the body of Charlotte Browne, cold and formidable under the shaven head, wide awake and angry. She plucks at her bandages. The wound burns like ice. A pink, floppy-breasted woman wearing lipstick is staring at her from the next-door bed. She smiles while readjusting the neckline of her pink nightie.

'Is there a telephone?' asks Charlotte.

'Yes,' smiles the pink woman, 'in the corridor, opposite the first of the men's wards.'

But then Charlotte remembers, she has no money, no hand-bag, no clothes. She opens her locker and looks inside. It's empty. Her anger with Jim Reese is infecting her wound and making her body ache.

'Was anyone here?' she asks the woman, 'A man?'

'Only the policeman. You were sleeping.'

'Policeman?'

'Yes.'

So the phone call is useless. She knows Jim has gone, gone heaven knows where, in spite of her will to give his life purpose and shape. Only her strength is left now and she senses that this has ebbed, like Samson's, with the shaving of her hair. She would like to kill Jim Reese, for the wounding, for his presumption that he could rob her of her will. She remembers triumphantly her drive in the dusk to the great manor smelling of polish and flowers; she remembers the pathetic whining of the old dog in the gunroom, then the feel and weight of the gun, the cottagey smell of the woollen balaclava with which she covered her face, and the scuttling obedience of the servile man, Garrod, going shivering before her down the cellar steps, opening the safe with the same timid hands that have worn gloves to preside at the gross and formal richness of Ascot dinners, Jubilee parties, election night suppers, standing to one side in his thick night attire, head sad and limp as her memory selects the items of greatest value and she arranges them unhurriedly in the big suitcase. She remembers her sorrow for Garrod as she sits him down on the polished parquet of the hall, gags him with a soft scarf and ropes him to the banisters with nylon sailcord. How long, she wonders, will he sit and mourn his failure to protect his employers' precious things? Before someone comes. A charwoman? A cleaning slave with a key? In her childhood, there were four living-in servants at Sowby. Time has passed. Sowby still stands, protected and protector, yet depleted. Charlotte drives fast away from it, away from the scent of catmint and childhood and trifling obedience to cruel ways. I, she says aloud as she flies down the chestnut avenue, have committed no crime. The fearful unkindnesses of genteel lives make wounds deeper than any I have inflicted. All I have done is to snatch the weapons of tomorrow – for use today. She feels then a rising in her of terrible excitement. She drives badly, blindly, fast, then she stops the car in a quiet lane, walks into the darkness and listens to the whispers of the momentous night. The past is dismembered, like a body, and inhabits only the space of a suitcase; the present is this warm, ripe darkness; the future is growing steadily in her and needs only the slow light of morning to begin.

Yet in the morning, the future changed. It was altered, as the future so very frequently is, by anger. The pink woman takes up some pink knitting. Charlotte senses that underneath the lump of bedclothes this woman is pregnant. She yawns at the terrible boredom of life's patterns. She curses the ebbing of strength. Jim Reese has beaten her, yet for what? For that drooling dog, pride? For that nameless stray, freedom? She sees his narrow white wrists on her bony shoulders, pressing her headful of understanding into his belly. Probably he loved no one, nor ever would, yet in her weakness, now, she begins to cry for the loss of him. She lies back on the clean pillows and lets her tears fall silently. The pink woman looks away. A ward sister appears at the door, unseen by Charlotte. The ward sister crosses to Charlotte's bed and, without speaking to her, draws the curtains round it. Charlotte stares at the flowery curtains and asks in a quiet voice to be left alone. The ward sister doesn't reply. She lifts Charlotte up and forward, plumps the pillows, sets her back on the plumped pillows and says coldly: 'Alright, Miss Browne. A police sergeant is here. I shall now permit him to question you.'

*

Having woken so early on the 'heavenly day', Amelia Browne feels tired by the long walk down from the Glochenspiel. Her lilac dress is now a little crumpled and there are moist patches under her arms which she feels are 'most dreadfully common'.

'You have a swim, Duffy dear,' she says in the cool of the hotel foyer, 'I think I'm going to have a bit of a rest.'

Colonel Browne knows he can snooze pleasantly in the sun by the pool, so he changes into his bathing trunks, takes his bathing towel and his airmail copy of the *Telegraph*, leaving his wife to rest her papery body in the silence of their room.

Amelia Browne doesn't sleep, however. She lies still and examines her thoughts for the source of a minute trembling of anxiety that flutters round her stomach. She thinks of her Duffy, his heavy body on the pool lounger, his bald head shiny as a conker in the late afternoon sun. She knows Duffy is alright. His war wound has been mercifully quiet lately; there has been no recurrence, thank heavens, of the prostate trouble which threatened a year ago. He is healthy and jolly and she loves him for his health and jollity. No, it isn't Duffy causing the anxiety. So she searches. For a brief and uncomfortable space of time, she summons Charlotte to her mind. The anxiety is not lessened nor satisfied. Yet Amelia Browne feels glad that she has allowed herself, in this cool, pretty room, to confront this strange and vexing only child, to look at her as she must be now after seven years of absence and seven grim years of silence. She cannot distort or change her picture of the golden hair that scarcely darkened after childhood. She cannot believe that this has altered. But the face? The face will have aged a little, grown more severe no doubt, just as, from the little she ever hears, the life is of horrendous severity, unimaginable, alien, discomforting and cruel.

Amelia's emotional repertoire is 'not up to tragedy', as she once wittily said while eating profiteroles at Government House, Rhodesia. If it were, she might place herself in the role of Lear, more sinned against than sinning by the fierce daughter she has never allowed herself to understand. She has, of course, asked the genial Duffy several times: 'Where did we go wrong, Duffy sweet?' But the Colonel mistrusts all analysis, philosophical and psychological in particular, so cannot answer this bewildering question, except to state: 'We're not the ones who *went* wrong, Amelia. Blame the reds. Blame the Trotskyites or the Mao Tse Tungites or the heaven-knows-whatites. But don't blame us.' Yet Amelia is not comforted. Her memory returns very often to a windy day at Broadstairs – or was it Woolacombe? – when some loathesome little boy stuck a metal spade into her daughter's thigh, and the wind took her cries out to sea as she sat with Duffy in the dunes, and when they came at last to the child, the sand was crimson with her blood. She blamed the wind for taking the crying away into the ocean. She blamed the Nanny for allowing the boy to stray from her side. She did not blame herself. But now she suspects, though she doesn't mention it to Duffy, that other wounds may have been inflicted on Charlotte without her noticing them. Certainly Rhodesia seemed to wound her daughter, though nobody could understand why when it was such a paradise then. But when asking to be flown back to England, Charlotte had used peculiar words: 'I want you to release me,' she had said.

The sun nears the edge of the mountain that will extinguish it. The Colonel gets up, feeling chilly, and goes back into the hotel. Amelia Browne sleeps at last for a short while.

*

And on the beach at Brighton, the sun is getting lower. Canvas windbreaks are tugged up and folded away. The tops of thermoses are screwed on. Children are held and dried. Out in the deep middle distance, a well fitted and elegant yacht makes headway in the evening offshore breeze. The captain and owner of this yacht is a ginger-haired bank manager called Owen Lasky. His wife, Jessica-Lee Lasky, is American by origin and still fond of cocktails. As Owen urges his boat towards the horizon, Jessica-Lee is hauling on ropes and thinking about manhattans.

Jim Reese is swimming. Brought up on the edge of that piece of ocean, sometime pale-limbed member of the Under Elevens Neptune Club, he swims well and strongly, enjoying the immensity of the water. Of water, of this sea, he wants to say: here is *my* element. He rolls onto his back and floats. The gentle swell is kinder to his head than any pillow or woman's breast because it moves him forward. Man breaks from the kind fluids of the womb and is dried and wrapped, tottering out his futile years on two dry legs. But the pain of those thousands of days of standing upright! The longings to lie down and be rocked by love or purpose or adulation! Earth. The wrong element. An evolutionary mistake. The root cause of all oppression and the abandonment of children in cupboard rooms smelling of damp laundry mangles and mothballs. WE ARE NOT PEOPLE OF DUST! He mouths this to the clear sky and the wind. A seagull shrieks. He sits up in the wonderful sea and it shows him the beach, grey-yellow, the white houses, the cliffs like crumbly coconut-ice. The people are not even blobs or dots. The people are not there.

So he lies back, comforted. Then he rolls over, holds the fathoms in his arms like a lover and each second the body he rides hurls him forward with its own changing shape. So begins the love affair of Jim Reese with the sea. As the sun sinks and the colours of the sun spread through the water, it grows more intense and harder to relinquish. From the stern of her husband's yacht, Jessica-Lee Lasky, holding an imaginary

cocktail glass in her left hand, sees it for one piercing second:
the flesh and dark head of Jim Reese embedded in the body of
the ocean. She calls to Owen Lasky: 'Owen! I saw a man!' And
Owen traipses to the jolting aft section of his boat and stares
with his wife at the empty water. They stare and stare.
Jessica-Lee Lasky forgets cocktails and starts to feel afraid.
Owen pats her shoulder and says in his bank manager's voice:
'You must have imagined him, dear.' But no, Jessica-Lee feels
certain that she saw him, this person holding fast to the water
itself as if to a raft, and asks her husband to turn the boat
round.

*

Detective Inspector Pitt and WPC Verna Willis have carried
Garrod to a bedroom which he, yet not they, recognises as
Colonel Browne's own bedroom. In this lofty bed, the old man
is becoming for the second time in his life the returning war
hero, the lad who showed courage and initiative, the lad who
came through . . .

'Sailcord,' he says in a disdainful, tired voice, 'she tied me
with sailcord. There's give in sailcord, you see, Sir.'

The ambulance has been called. WPC Willis, who did a
year's nursing training before she joined the force, has taken
Garrod's pulse and listened to his heart and both these mani-
festations of life are fluttery and feeble. She looks concerned as
Pitt ploughs on with his questions.

'Did you recognise the woman?'

'No, Sir.'

'We have reason to believe the woman was Colonel
Browne's daughter.'

'I never met the daughter. I came to this house in '76. She
was on the television that year or the next. Some demonstra-
tion. She had red hair. But I never met her.'

'But this woman was about her age, was she?'

'I don't know, Inspector. Her face was covered. And the
hair.'

'How had she got into the house?'

'Well. She walked in. There wasn't any noise.'

'So she had a key to the front door?'

'I reckon.'

'The door wasn't bolted?'

Garrod winces. Now the returning war hero remembers the unfastened safety catch on the rifle, the puncture in the spare tyre of the jeep . . . The circling bird begins its far off turning and Garrod is silent.

'Mr Garrod? Was the front door not bolted?'

Garrod's head lolls. He whispers: 'Dunno how she could have known . . . '

'Known?'

'I've been ill, Sir. Laid up.'

'And you believe the woman knew this?'

'Or I would have remembered the door . . . '

'The bolt?'

'Yes. I would have remembered the bolt.'

Detective Inspector Pitt looks at WPC Willis, who has turned on a little green-shaded lamp in the darkening bedroom. Pitt has, in twenty-two years with the police, never felt comfortable with remorse. His look is a signal for Willis to take up the questioning.

'How long has Colonel Browne been away, Mr Garrod?'

'Oh. A fortnight. Thereabouts. They've gone for three weeks – to Switzerland.'

'And is it possible that Miss Browne was told about their holiday?'

'I don't think so. She wasn't told what they did.'

'Perhaps they go away every year at this time, do they?'

'Now abouts. Lady Amelia loves the Alps. In summer.'

*

And Garrod is right. Amelia Browne does love to gaze, as she gazes now, at the first stars peeping through their light years at her scented body on the hotel balcony and sense the now unseen presence of the mountains shouldering off the sky. She has dined well. At dinner, Duffy made a very un-Duffyish little speech about companionship and love, and his reassuring large presence at her side, coupled with these resonant words, have helped to quell the flutter of anxiety she had earlier struggled with. She has made no attempt, although it occurred to her to do so, to talk to Duffy about Charlotte. In spite of her protected life, Amelia Browne is like a patient birdwatcher of suffering. She detects it where others detect nothing. And in the spreading woods and rambly thickets of her husband's con-

tented life she has often seen it, the camouflaged frail body of
the bird, suffering. It has built nests in the once radiant part of
him, in foliage the colour of her daughter's hair. But he isn't a
wordy man. Duffy and words seem to be locked in a lifelong
struggle – an iguana fighting with the Shorter Oxford English
Dictionary. So he has never been able to say that Charlotte has
made him suffer, nor how, nor why. 'I just don't think about
her, Amelia,' he once snapped into his glass of port. Then
drained the glass like a bitter draught. And Amelia saw it:
some cuckoobird quite alien to him, yet lodged there, and in
certain seasons repetitively calling.

Now he lies in the hotel bed, reading a new book about the
Falklands War and waiting for Amelia to come in off the
balcony. Slightly over-fed, he is content and sleepy. He
admires Amelia for admiring the stars. He is indifferent to
stars. He is beginning, lazily, to wonder what gulfs of the spirit
still separate him from Amelia when the telephone at his elbow
jolts him into concerned wakefulness. He picks up the receiver.
Amelia's face appears at the window and stares at him. From
far away under the mountains, a dry English voice speaks in a
tunnel of silence:

'Colonel Browne?'

'Yes.'

Amelia slips into the room. She presses a thin hand to her top
lip.

'Detective Inspector Pitt, CID, here, Sir. I'm calling from
Sowby.'

*

It is morning. Doyle has slept well. He congratulates himself
on his refusal to dream about Margaret. He feels well in his
new blood.

He hears nurses' voices whispering together over their
dispensary trolley. He hears the words police . . . revolutionary . . . press . . . story . . . His scriptwriter's heart pauses in its
pumping to let these words stream through him like plasma.
He feigns sleep. The nurses' hands continue to measure out
pills in little beakers. But over this measuring comes the almost
inaudible conversation, patchy, like the shading of a face
before the features are pencilled in:

'Someone . . . hospital . . . told the newspapers . . .'

'Sister Osborne . . . night duty . . . '

'The same policeman?'

'Yes.'

' . . . in Alexandra Ward . . . '

'Yes?'

'Charlotte Browne.'

Now they are at Doyle's bed.

'Mr Doyle . . .'

He opens his eyes and smiles at the nurses.

'Sleep well, Mr Doyle?'

'Yes. I didn't dream, thank heavens.'

A thermometer is stuck into his mouth. One of the nurses examines the chart at the end of his bed, looks at Doyle, looks back at the chart. Doyle, silenced by the thermometer, wants to compliment them on the quality of the new blood they have given him. He has been replenished with curiosity.

The thermometer is taken out, held, shaken, replaced in a glass of disinfectant. Doyle awaits pills in a red beaker, but he's given none and the nurses pass away from him, still whispering.

When they leave the ward, Doyle gets out of bed and stands up. In the bed next to his, a bald man who has dreams of tap-dancing is inserting his morning teeth. Doyle walks quietly over the lino to the swing doors of his ward, then out into the wide hygenic corridor where an Indian woman is polishing the floor.

'Alexandra Ward?' he asks.

The Indian woman, with a jewel-pierced nose, is a stooped and slow person. She examines Doyle's bandaged arm, his hospital nightshirt, his hirsute legs beneath.

'Left,' she says blankly.

Doyle nods, turns left into an identical corridor. No one sees him yet. He comes to a waiting area, where plastic chairs of the kind which creaked under the pelvis of Sergeant McCluskie are lined up in two rows. To his left, now, he sees a green and white sign saying Alexandra Ward, Princess Anne Ward, Edith Cavell Ward. He has come to the women's territory.

He hears footsteps approaching the reception area. Without hesitation, he opens the swing doors to Alexandra Ward and finds himself in a shadowy room, where the patients are still sleeping.

But at the far end of the room, he recognises her – the only one awake and staring at the window. He knows the name, the voice, the profile. He has even read her book, with its preposterous title, *The Salvation of Man*. The minute he sees her, he feels excitement stir, shamefaced, under the ludicrous night garment. He moves gravely towards her. She is, he summarises, one of the stars of dissent.

Still no one discovers him. The pink woman sleeps with her cherub mouth wide and her knitting folded on her feet. All the other Alexandrine women sleep, rasping through the discomforts of the short night. Only Charlotte sees him now, ridiculous in his gown, unshaven, pale and wild. She isn't afraid. Charlotte is seldom afraid. She wants to laugh. He reminds her of a younger Jack Lemmon. Any minute, she knows, he will be carried off by the day-shift nurses beginning duty.

But the day-shift nurses allotted to Alexandra Ward are busy elsewhere. Burn victims of a tenement fire are being wheeled, screaming, into the hospital. Nurses are running, surgeons are hauled from sleep, lights are going on in ante-rooms and operating rooms, vents hiss and blow, in the sluice rooms water gushes. And so it is because of a fire, in which two people will have died, because of Sergeant McCluskie's need to open his bowels after his dreary, caffeinated night, that Franklin Doyle is able to walk out of his ward and into Charlotte's ward and sit on her bed for four minutes before McCluskie returns, sees him and hauls him away.

'You're Charlotte Browne . . . ' he whispers lamely.

She nods, lazily. In this one, unfrightened gesture, she has accepted the stranger on her bed.

'Franklin Doyle,' he states hurriedly, 'scriptwriter, film-maker, bum . . . '

She smiles. In the grey light, she is superb.

'I dare say that policeman will remove you.'

Doyle ignores this, hurries on: 'Why are the press interested this time?'

'Are they?'

'I heard the press are here.'

'They may be. They're always interested.'

'What have you done, Charlotte?'

'Something. So I'll do a stretch this time. Long.'

'Want to tell it to someone who gets it right?'

'To a bum?'

'Sure. Who better?'

'Then you find Jim Reese for me.'

'Jim Reese.'

'He might be in Brighton. Look there first. He's a drummer, or was. Thirty-seven. Dark. Very thin. Wearing a vest probably. I expect there's a warrant out. Try to find him first.'

'Okay. Sure . . . I . . . who is he to you?'

'No one any more. But if you find him, tell him love is probably stronger than springs.'

'*Springs?*'

'Yes.'

'Spring as in the season?'

'No. As in a coil of wire.'

'With what significance?'

'Just tell him – if you find him. And then,' she looks away from him at the day beginning at the window and yawns, 'you can tell everyone else the story, I suppose: I stole, but I stole nothing of true value. The true value of what I stole would have appeared in the currency I was going to convert it to. The owners of these so-called valuables are my parents. Neither of these people, my parents, have *ever* offered anything of themselves for the good of anyone but themselves. Even now, their selfishness is intact, so I've taken nothing from them. I carried a gun – my father's, used to kill game for sport – but I wounded no one. Only myself. My sense of obedience which I tried to extinguish long ago had refused to die utterly, until now. I think it's dead now. Yet its death wounds. Do you see? In a newly ordered world, I would be obedient to the law. I am, always have been, obedient to love. In a peaceful world, I would keep the peace.'

Charlotte pauses, looks away from Doyle, who is trembling.

'Do you expect to be understood?' he asks.

She smiles. The smile is gentle and sad. 'No.'

'By a few?'

'Do *you* understand?'

'Why did you need the gun? If it was your parents' house . . .?'

'There's a servant there. He wasn't harmed. He has the key to the safe.'

'And your headwound?'

'Nothing. I fell down some basement steps.'

'Did the servant try to defend the house?'

'No.'

'Did you act entirely by yourself?'

'Oh yes.'

'Jim Reese wasn't part of it?'

Charlotte turns away again and stares at the cracks of light in the blinds. The day will be hot again. A heatwave is coming. As Charlotte, child, she climbs to the orchard at Sowby. The ancient gardener with his black-creased hands lifts her high into a plum tree. The plum she choses with her chubby hand is half eaten away by wasps.

'What organisation are you working for now, Charlotte?'

'Many.'

'Is Jim Reese part of an organisation?'

'No.'

'Jim Reese is not working with you?'

'No. He needed my help. I thought he did.'

'With what? With a political set-up?'

'No. He just used me as a shroud.'

'A *what?*'

'Over his past.'

Disturbed by the voices, the pink woman has woken. She is gawping with round scared eyes at Doyle and Charlotte and pressing her buzzer that will summon a nurse. Doyle feels dismay as acute as grief at the ending of this meeting.

'Charlotte. Can I come and see you in prison?'

'You won't be allowed.'

'If I find a way?'

She smiles again, touches his hand lightly. Then, with loathing, she whispers: 'It might be ten years.'

'No. No one was hurt. It won't be . . .'

It takes Sergeant McCluskie and Staff Nurse Beckett less than ten seconds to cross the ward and seize Doyle by his arms. In their zeal to remove him, they forget the deep wound in his right arm, and as they lead him back to his ward it begins to bleed afresh.

*

In brilliant early morning sunshine, the hired car takes Colonel and Lady Amelia Browne down and down the mountain to the waiting plane. Neither has slept for long. They wear their sunglasses and sit in silence behind the Swiss chauffeur who drives with ease and politeness, trying not to jolt his passengers from side to side on the sharp corners.

As they leave the mountains and the road straightens monotonously, Amelia brings out a little scented handkerchief, blows her nose and sighs: 'What an end, Duffy.'

Duffy coughs. His military mind had planned their holiday with the precision of a campaign. To sacrifice seven and a half days of that campaign has annoyed him deeply. And all night his mind has repeated the clipped utterances of Detective Inspector Pitt. Pitt – 'whoever this damn Pitt is!' – also annoys him deeply, because he, who prides himself on his knowledge of men, has marked Pitt for a dissembler. 'You see,' he explains now to Amelia, 'the British police are utterly bamboozled in ninety per cent of British robberies, Amelia. They have no more clue as to who did what than your average orang-utang, your average Maasai warrior. Less, in fact. But in this case, Pitt *knows*.'

'Knows what, Duffy?'

'He's trying to pretend he doesn't, but he does.'

'Does what?'

'He knows who broke into Sowby. He just isn't saying.'

'Why not?'

'That's precisely it, Amelia.'

'Well, I can't see that it matters much who did it. They say they've found the paintings and the jewellery, thank goodness.'

'So why is Pitt insisting that we cut short our holiday?'

'Well, poor Garrod. They want to stop this kind of thing happening again.'

'Oh don't be silly, Amelia.'

'Well, how do I know, Duffy?'

'You mean you haven't been working it out?'

'Working what out?'

'Who robbed us.'

'How could I work it out? That's the job of Pitt, or whatever he's called. And I'm not even in England.'

'I've worked it out.'

'I can't imagine how.'

'It all fits: Pitt's lying, the summons home . . .'

'What fits?'

'It was Charlotte.'

Amelia is rigid in the car. Her mouth is a little scar of puckered lines. Duffy looks away from this petrified face. Yet he feels relief. She had to know. He, not the policeman, had to be the one to tell her.

Minutes pass. The car sways on. Lush fields flank the road. Amelia blinks and blinks behind her glasses. No, she promises herself, this can't be right. Because this would be it – the ending. The ending she has feared for years, the ending like a death, the death of all hope that the child she brought up in an English paradise would come home to thank her and save her. Save her from what?

'Ohh . . . ' she wails, 'Ohh, Duffy . . . '

From guilt.

From her terrible neglect.

From the useless buying of bronze statuettes.

From the language of cliché and cruelty.

From flower arrangements and servants.

From indifference.

From her proud blood . . .

'Ohh . . . Duffy . . . I simply cannot believe that . . . '

Duffy puts a wide hand out to Amelia. He feels lumpen with dread, in need of comfort himself.

'I could be wrong, old thing,' he says in a choked voice.

So of course, in her agony, Amelia is cross: 'Then why on earth did you even suggest it? How could you imagine Charlotte doing a thing like this? She's not a criminal!'

Duffy sighs, removes the gift of his pink hand.

'In this society,' he says slowly, 'she is.'

*

Death. As she leaves the hospital in the police car, Charlotte has not imagined death. To Jim Reese, she had wanted to offer a birthright. This offered birthright would, she had decided, engender a birth: a birth of self-respect, a birth of energy and purpose. In other words, a new life. Because in the basement rooms Jim Reese was sinking, fading, disappearing. In his fingers, in his knuckles, rhythms of his onetime visibility were occasionally heard. But, parted from the drums, from the absolution of his own music, he was thinning, flaking, becoming opaque. How many people, Charlotte wonders, as the police car passes the Camden Plaza showing a black and white Italian film, are obscured by their own uselessness?

She hasn't 'saved' Jim Reese. Pride and anger prevented this. She is punished for her arrogance. And he, in the flood of his male violence, has rendered her useless to the women she has worked with, worked for, when to them too she planned to offer more, on this Buckinghamshire night, than an act of daring. They will come to her in prison, she knows. In their tattered layers of clothes, some with backpacked babies, some spikey and pale in their fierce lesbian love affairs, some weathered and worn into grannies, somebody's kindly nan in a woollen hat, holding a banner while the relations sneer and gasp at her picture on the nine o'clock news . . . They will circle outside the prison gates, sparrows of women, ravens of women, women with their dreams of peace. With the gold and the silver, they would have printed leaflets, bought newspaper space, funded crèches, financed a conference. Now, nothing is left for them from Charlotte, only her presence, soon, in the massive prison and the story of her crime, falling on them, asking them to stand responsible.

Charlotte is quiet as the car stops and starts in the dense morning traffic. She sends away her sad thoughts of women and focuses instead on the stranger at the foot of her bed, the man Doyle with his wounded arm. Laughingly, she imagines him travelling to the south coast in search of Jim Reese, wearing his hospital nightie. He has become precious to her because he, in all the questioning to come, will be her only secret.

But secret deaths are occurring. Unplanned. Unexpected. Handcuffed to WPC Beckett, Charlotte walks up the steps of the police station. At the same moment, her solicitor, Mr Charles Ogden-Nichols, locks the driver's door of his BMW and prepares to walk into a limelight he has coveted for some years. At the same moment, Garrod dies.

Garrod dies. The struggle of his hands with a tangle of nylon sailcord is not unconnected with his death. While his hands struggled, his veteran's heart made a salient in death's lines. A few hours later, the salient became a bridgehead and his life goes teeming, streaming across the bridgehead, past and fast over the no man's land of imaginary desert and tanks like mice, racing to death as if his own spirit were death's batman. In the grounds of Sowby Manor, where a young constable called Arthur Williams is walking in Lady Amelia's rose garden with Admiral, the dog pricks up its ears and lets out a peculiar whine. PC Williams jerks at its lead. Lady Amelia's roses are funnelled by bees. A nurse comes running to the straight green line which is the technological death of Garrod. His desert is at last deserted.

Within hours, news of Garrod's death reaches Camden Police Station. Charles Ogden-Nichols looks grave in the manner of an idle poet as he privately notes that the charge will now be manslaughter. Charlotte is closed like a mollusc with her thoughts of prison-death. Months. Years. Prison-cancer. Release at fifty, old, obese, corrupted, idle, finished. And for what? It was fine, of course, the night of stars, the glint of flowers as she went in, the white face of the Duke of Abercorn watching her through time . . . And the Colonel is punished, her mother is punished at last – for their hearts empty of love and their heads full of silver knives and paperweights. Yet once more, because of them, she will be locked away. As a child, it was her head they imprisoned with sighings after royalty and debutante balls; now it is her body.

Charlotte sits. They allow her to sit. Already, Ogden-Nichols is composing the stirring sonnets of her case. He smiles at her, but she looks away. He and she are given cups of tea.

*

And at their Brighton mooring, Owen Lasky and his wife, Jessica-Lee, clamber out of their foam rubber bunks, twitch their elasticated curtains to let in a shaft of sun and put on their tin kettle to make coffee.

Until it was dark, they turned their boat in wider and wider circles, searching for the body of the man Jessica-Lee had seen for less than a second, lying with his mouth in the waves. Owen grumbled. What a stupid waste of time, this making of circles. But Jessica-Lee would not let them go back till they were dizzy and tired with their turning in the wind and all the lights had come on in the town. Then they limped in, moored the boat, took down the sails, went to their favourite pub to forget. Owen drank beer. Jessica-Lee drank gin fizzes. That night, they had dreams of Miami.

Jim Reese saw the boat. He saw it tack and turn, tack and turn. He knew that for the second time in twenty-four hours someone was trying to save him with clumsy, futile action. He laughed aloud in the gathering dusk, the laughter and the body that housed it still strong, still riding the water like a lover. He knew that the boat wouldn't find him. Darkness and his sea would cover and conceal him.

He remembered the exploding toys of John Ripley. One was a boat. You assembled it, piece by piece, deck by deck, around a central spring. You aimed amidships with your three-inch lead-painted torpedo. The boat burst into satisfactory fragments on the hearth rug. John Ripley laughed. Mother screamed a little scream. John Ripley said, don't worry lad, the whole point is you can't break it. You put it back together and then you have another go. Easy. Doddle! Like this, around the central spring . . .

The central spring . . . ? The boat tacks, turns . . . Lights come on in it. The central spring will, if you aim too often and over and over again at the area of greatest weakness . . . yes, even there on the hearth rug in front of the brittle white tubes of the gas fire . . . right there, with Mother looking on, arms folded, hip slightly jutted to one side, makeup on, smelling of Blue Grass . . . there, where all had once seemed so exceptionally safe and familiar and comforting and eternal . . . *there*, the central spring will one day snap. Yet all continues to tack, to turn, to make its habitual movement, just as if nothing had occurred. No one but you perceives that the spring is broken. You reassemble the boat. The boat is whole, deck on deck. Merely, it will no longer explode when hit. And Mother takes up the tea cosy stained by her greasy hands, pops it over the brown pot, struts out into the hall and calls John Ripley down to tea. You leave the dead toy on the hearth rug. You sit at the table and watch their mouths, runny with egg, oily with bacon. They talk and laugh and gobble and suck their tea. You want to say to them, the central spring went. You take a breath, to begin. Before any words come out, Mother reprimands you with her eyes: you have ceased to matter.

When the boat gave up its useless search and returned to harbour, the great depths of the sea began to beat like music in the ears of Jim Reese. The music invaded him, commanding his hands, his arms, his legs, his pelvis to keep time. Water streamed off his forehead and into his hair. The cold of the ocean became, with its new rhythm, a fierce heat. Never had movement been so exquisite a thing. Never in the turning multicoloured lights and the screaming dreams of Vegas had body and music been one as they were now one. And Jim Reese knew that it would last forever. The sky would fill with stars and it would go on and on. Dawn would come and daybreak and autumn and sighing and sunset, and still it would play. Because it was his. His own.

*

Franklin Doyle discharges himself from hospital and goes home to his flat. On the mat is a note in Margaret's handwriting. He picks it up, almost without curiosity, and takes it to his desk, where he telephones a glazier and asks for someone to come and mend his window.

Mrs Annipavroni had cleaned out the cat litter tray and scrubbed with Flash and Vim at the bloodstains on the kitchen floor. The whole flat smells of Vim. But it is tidy and quiet. Doyle re-enters it with a feeling of gratefulness. He telephones a florist and orders carnations and cornflowers to be sent to Kilburn, to Julietta Annipavroni, whose address begins: 'Staircase B'. He feels grateful, too, that his own address doesn't begin with Staircase B. He imagines the Annipavroni family lugging their Italian life up and down dark concrete steps.

Doyle pours himself fresh orange juice and sits, stroking the cat. He ignores Margaret's note on the desk. His head is crammed with half-formed plans, jostling each other for place and meaning. His wound throbs. He is sweating slightly. He has a sudden longing to sleep. He imagines Charlotte's cold strong hands holding his head and laying it gently on her shoulder. She becomes the man, he the woman, content to lie safely at her side. He sleeps and offers himself. She is aloof in her hard body. She crushes him with her indifference, but his yearnings for her only increase.

The telephone wakes him. As he walks to the desk, he knows he has dreamed of Charlotte, yet the dream has left him. All he wants to hear, as he lifts the receiver, is Charlotte's voice. He is aware, in this instant, that he has fallen in love.

Margaret sounds close, as if she were calling from an adjoining room. She's been with Michael, she says. She thought she loved Michael, yet in his room, right there in his bed, she began to remember Doyle . . .

'Oh, Margaret . . . ' Doyle's voice is weary, irritated, 'please don't bug me with this kind of thing.'

'But it happened, Franklin. I wasn't consciously thinking about you and I suddenly started to miss you and regret – '

'Regret what?'

'I don't think I can leave you.'

'You've left me. You left me!'

'I know. But it's all wrong.'

Doyle sighs. He looks at his wound. Yesterday, he might have died for Margaret. Now, already, he has replaced her.

'I think I need both of you, Franklin. Can you understand this? Franklin?'

'Oh bullshit.'

'What? I can't hear you, Franklin. Did you hear what I said about needing you both?'

He says nothing. His wound aches. He must buy painkillers. Then his dream comes back to him. He lies, arms and legs spread wide, and Charlotte's body is above him, moving gently, purposefully, yet almost invisibly in near darkness. Then she lowers her head and whispers to his mouth: 'This isn't love. I'm giving you blood, that's all.'

'Franklin? Are you there?'

'Yeah.'

'I know it's difficult for you. Can I come round and talk to you?'

Doyle isn't concentrating. The pain of Charlotte in him is as acute as the pain of his unhealed arm.

'I'm sorry . . . ' he mumbles.

'Can't I come round?'

'I'm sorry, Margaret. Things have happened. I'm going to have to be away for a bit.'

'I could come round now, Franklin. We need to talk.'

'No. I'm sorry.'

'Why d'you keep saying you're sorry? I'm the one – '

'Yes, I know. I'll send on the things I didn't pack for you.'

He hangs up. He knows this is cowardly. He knows she will ring back. He goes quickly to the kitchen, opens a tin of food for the cat, then grabs a clean jacket from his wardrobe and a pad from the desk. His head is clearing now. He has set the visit to Brighton aside, because he doesn't want to go in search of Charlotte's lover: he needs Charlotte herself.

As he closes the flat door, he hears the telephone begin to ring. The sound follows him down the stairs. But moments later he has escaped it. He is out in the hot day. In the street, the air is warm and rich with the smell of privet. Sun gleams on the white fronts of houses and London is transformed into a kindly city. Doyle hails a taxi. His heart races with the engine as it whisks him towards the police station where, already, the reporters have begun to gather, and crews from the BBC and London Weekend Television are setting up cameras.

*

News is travelling in spirals and loops. Charlotte Browne, celebrity revolutionary, is for the third time in her life under arrest. The BBC's Home Affairs Correspondent, tanned from a holiday rather far from home, prepares to pass on to the nation facts known and unknown concerning the charges. Here, procrastination by the police is impeding the swift passage of information to the public at large, a public who, within a few hours, will know that Charlotte has robbed the house of her parents and been responsible for the death of an elderly servant. Reporters and camera crews shuffle and smoke and buy cheese sandwiches from Vincente's sandwich shop and wait in sprawled groups. Passers by, sensing life altering here in a Camden street, hang around to marvel or condemn. They are joined by Doyle, who thrusts himself forward, holding high his bandaged arm like a white flag and pleads with the nervous-seeming constable on the door to be allowed to see Charlotte. His subterfuge – that he is Charlotte's fiancé – is merely smiled upon. Up and down the country, police are looking for Jim Reese. Even the PC at the station door knows that this middle-aged American is not Jim Reese. Doyle is turned away.

And then, in an hour, the news of the tumbling ashore of the drowned body of Jim Reese comes echoing down the telephone. The fact is as yet kept hidden from Doyle and the gathered reporters. The fact is as yet kept hidden from Detective Inspector Pitt who waits at Sowby for the afternoon arrival of Colonel and Lady Amelia Browne. It is given, however, to Detective Chief Superintendent Bowden, the man who, with the facts of Charlotte's case slowly accumulating, is now 'in charge'. Bowden is a lofty, remote man, with a thin moustache and flinty eyes. Articulate and bitter, he's known as a hard-liner. His favourite meal is shepherd's pie. Whenever he eats this dish, he takes pleasure in the picture that he conjures of his wife sitting down all day to grind lamb through the mincer. Bowden dislikes women. He makes love to his wife no more than six or seven times a year. Women like Charlotte he would willingly see hanged. What repulses him most about her in particular is her dignity.

So now he walks to her cell, where she and Ogden-Nichols are for the moment sitting in silence. Ogden-Nichols's long poet's face is gloomy with certainty; for all his cleverness, for all the limelight that will spill onto his carpeted office in Queen Anne Street, he knows he will fail to alter the verdict of the trial to come.

Charlotte's cell is unlocked for Bowden. He stares icily at her, sitting straight and calm on the hard bed. Ogden-Nichols stands up as he comes in. Charlotte doesn't move. Bowden gestures to Ogden-Nichols to leave the cell. Charlotte, for the very first time since she drove to Buckinghamshire, feels a tremor of fear. Ogden-Nichols senses it too. Something has happened.

Bowden knows that Ogden-Nichols is entitled to stay. He knows also that he will leave. Now, he is alone with Charlotte, face to face. She puts her hands round her knees, calming her fear with this quiet rearrangement of her physical strength. She is like the leopard or the lioness, Bowden privately decides: she is savage.

He tugs out a packet of cigarettes and offers her one. She refuses. He puts the cigarettes back in his pocket, but doesn't sit down, as she expects him to. He stands, folds his arms, clears his throat, announces: 'Mr Reese has been found drowned at Brighton.'

Charlotte looks away from him, down at her hands. The knuckles are white, transparent she thinks, showing me the bone, the miraculous interior structure of me that will not decay when the flesh is gone. I must not allow myself to imagine the body of Jim on the sand. I must put the death aside and only fill my mind with this picture of hands – mine on his living body, touching, taking, soothing, his on my face and in my hair and on my breasts and at last in their ecstacy on the skin of the drums . . .

'We have positive identification of the body, and we are assuming suicide.'

Suicide. Of course, suicide.

Well, come to me, she thinks, the women who light their communal fires on perimeter railings, the hard and gentle women with their banners and their protestations, come and absolve me of my failure and my trust in a man. So she is quiet, imagining the gathering of this precious congregation. She still stares at her hands and doesn't even move her head to look up at Bowden. He stands and waits. He unfolds his arms, puts them behind his back. I have, he thinks, enjoyed every syllable inflicted here. But he is waiting for the physical show of shock and grief. He needs these. He won't be cheated of them. 'Come on, you cunt!' he wants to yell at her, 'start crying!'

But still he waits and waits. Far away in Charlotte's mind, the bones of hundreds of women, still fleshed out and lit with life, begin to gather in clusters.

*

'Poems, Duffy. Do you remember, she used to send us poems from boarding school?'

'Did she?'

'They were all about quite sentimental kinds of things, like dead baby birds.'

'Don't think I read them.'

'Yes you did, Duffy.'

'Dead birds?'

'That kind of thing. A lot of death.'

'Trouble with my daughter, she's always considered herself clever.'

They are alone now. They are home. The bar of light glows over the white forehead of the Duke of Abercorn. Duffy has poured them strong drinks. It is the hour when Garrod would have entered the sitting room quietly, either to announce dinner or carrying their television suppers on identical trays. At Amelia's feet, Admiral is sleeping. His flank trembles and twitches in his old dog's dreaming. Amelia stares down at the dog. He is ancient, she notices suddenly, and smelly and weak. Age creeps on invisible, until one day . . .

'I'd like to die, Duffy.'

She hasn't wept. She has held herself as cold and straight as an icicle. Her behaviour has won her the admiration of Pitt and of WPC Willis, whose cups of tea Amelia has stubbornly refused. But now she is alone. The truth of what has happened enters valves and arteries and begins to surge and stream through her. She gulps whisky, as if to dilute the truths inside her. Duffy stares at her: Amelia de Palfrey, great-niece of the seventh Duke of Abercorn, and what a slim beauty once, in her white gloves, smelling of pear blossom and gardenias . . .

'Don't talk bunkum like that, Amelia.'

'Though we ought to do something about flowers.'

'What flowers?'

'For Garrod. There should be a wreath. Something to lay on.'

'Don't worry about it, old thing.'

'You'll organise it.'

'Yes.'

'And one for me?'

'We can send one, Amelia, from us both.'

'I didn't say *from* me. I said *for* me.'

She dismays him now. Amelia de Palfrey. What an ideal wife she has made him over all the years. So good at choosing and arranging and reordering; she has furnished his entire existence. A simple man, he thinks, I am at heart a simple man and Amelia has perfectly understood me. Even at Christmas, in her choice of beige cashmere, she has never erred and in her peculiar love of mountains she has lifted me up.

'I think,' he says earnestly, 'we have to put all these tragedies out of our minds, Amelia, and try to go on as before.'

She doesn't answer. Her face looks slack, flattened almost, rearranged by some brutal palm.

'Amelia?'

'They were all about death.'

'What were?'

'Her poems. The deaths of one thing or another.'

'Stop it, Amelia! Got to keep a grip.'

The dog is woken by Duffy's voice. It gets to its feet and shakes itself. 'Siddown Admiral!' Duffy snaps.

Amelia pats the dog's head. It is, perhaps, the only thing left in need of her protection. Then she lifts her head and looks out.

The evening is deep blue at the window and the room is getting dark. She remembers the day the rose garden was planted and a pedestal built for the sundial. How old was Charlotte then, she wonders. Four? Five? Too small to understand the symmetry of a rose garden. The child used to scrunch the perfect blooms in her fat little hand.

The sky is darkening, too, over Camden. The reporters have gone, notebooks and spools of film replete with facts released by the woman-loathing Bowden, too late for the nine o'clock news. In the morning, the popular dailies will lead with the story, in which they have already taken sides. Editors in search of imagery will invoke serpents' teeth and thankless children, the while aware of the gulf separating their readership from a work of literature Amelia Browne had only inadequately understood. Charlotte is friendless, alone with the suicide of Jim Reese. His death binds and binds her head, like her bandage. She refuses the supper brought to her. She can't eat while the body of her lover is unburied. Yet, like her mother silently taking leave of her senses in an armchair by an unlit fire, she doesn't weep. She has seen the challenge in Bowden's eyes. She will not cry. If she is alone with the drowned limbs of Jim Reese, so too is she alone with her strength. Jim has failed her. She will not fail herself. When, near dawn, she sleeps, she dreams of Sowby. Her parents, manacled together by the handles of their tennis rackets, go wading into the lily pond like adventurous boys. Goldfish and newts nose their legs, but they stand very still at the pond's centre, holding up their skirts and trousers with their free hands.

*

Margaret has telephoned Doyle twice since he returned to the flat, hungry and excited. He has answered neither call. Into his Answerphone she has stammered out messages of her confusion.

Doyle has visited an all-hours delicatessen, bought himself sesame bread, Russian salad, Italian salami and a bottle of wine and has eaten these watching the ten o'clock news, on which the first mention of Charlotte's crime appears, well supported with photographs and information about her involvement with pacifist and feminist groups and her previous convictions.

Doyle crosses the room and catches sight of himself in a gold-framed mirror. His beard is as long as the stubble growing through on Charlotte's head, his eyes are vast and bright, his cheeks are blotchy and feverish. Round his neck is the white sling which carries his arm. The ancient mariner slung with the albatross? The comparison slips into his mind and stays there while he stares at his altered image. The weariness in his limbs, the throbbing of his wound, the astonishing clarity of his eyes: all suggest some kind of journey. His rational self, the lazy, cautious Franklin Doyle, argues for sleep and rest. But he ignores the lazy, the rational. He simply removes himself from his own sight and goes almost hurriedly to his desk, where he sits down and begins to write. In no more than a few minutes, he covers a page with a minutely perceived description of Charlotte, focusing on the heaviness of her eyes, the seeming hard strength of her body, the wide spread of her hands. But then he sits back, gulps wine, slows his breathing, forces himself to think not of Charlotte but of himself. 'Exile (Voluntary. American),' he begins, 'Finds himself at centre of case which will shock this nation (in ways particular to this nation and its class system) more than far more terrible things, i.e. deaths in Lebanon. Or so I predict. Propose – yes, I do propose – to put myself in major role (for first time in life) in historic circumstance. Ways to go about this must include a) Visit to parents, b) Visit to parents of Jim Reese, if alive, c) Visit to all groups C. has worked or is working for, d) Access to press archives, e) Seeking legal ways to gain access to C. (NB phone Bob Mandlebaum). Eventual aim must be saleable screenplay and/or book like Mailer and Schiller's *Executioner's Song*.

But here he stops writing. He knows why he feels like a traveller, pain, excitement, fear, mingling in his blood. He knows why he will stay awake till dawn, planning, constructing, ignoring calls on his Answerphone, disdaining sleep: he has entered on the most perfect love affair of his life. In Charlotte, he has found both woman and livelihood, fortuitously joined. Charlotte Browne is not only herself, but her story. Her story will become his. He will make the two inseparable. It doesn't concern Franklin Doyle on this long summer night that Charlotte the woman has, by giving him this story, put herself beyond the reach of his body. Because his body, with its disappointments of forty-seven years, is already

44

anointed by the brief touch of her in the hospital bed and he will not be denied her. She will be locked away from him, but he will remake her. To Charlotte, prisoner, he will offer the story of Charlotte; in Charlotte, remade as fiction, will he spend his love.

The wine is gone. Doyle goes to the kitchen, hauls out an opened bottle of cheap retsina. With this beginning to slide through his excited blood, he returns to his description of Charlotte. After a while, he abandons it again, continues his note-making, then stops suddenly and looks up. He reminds himself that all, *all* that is now taking place is taking place because of the interception of Julietta Annipavroni, once beautiful Italian girl, now struggling through middle age 'saving the lives' of those rich enough to pay her two pounds an hour. He smiles, remembering the flowers he has sent; Julietta Annipavroni arranges them in a vast green vase, won at a funfair. The blue of the cornflowers reminds her of the sky above Naples. 'Don't touch them!' she yells at her children.

Like Charlotte, prisoner, Doyle sleeps at dawn. The sun comes up on London. The same sounds of blackbirds trilling in cherry trees, so lately heard by Jim Reese in a basement flat, begin in the street, but Doyle is dreaming of fame and money and does not hear them.

Wedding Night

At the time of my father's second wedding, we lived in Paris, in a house a little grander than we could afford. It was the kind of house, in the Avenue Foch, which is today divided up very profitably and let as luxury flats. It seems astonishing to me now that our family once owned the whole of it. The drawing room, I recall, was on the first floor. Two sets of French windows led out from it onto small balconies. On these extremely pretty balconies my mother had always placed stone pots of geraniums. Well, in summer she had, I suppose. Geraniums don't survive winters, do they? It was high summer when my father got married for the second time, and I know that, by then, there weren't any geraniums on the drawing-room balconies.

I have always remembered the details of things, especially of rooms where I've lived. My brother does this too: together, we can reconstruct places, object by object. I think this gift or skill of ours is not really a gift or skill at all, but merely a habit into which, as soon as we could talk, we were obliged to fall: because our father was blind. He was blind by the time we were born and he never saw us. He saw our mother for one year of their married life, and I must say that she honestly was, at that time, one of the most beautiful women I have ever seen. Well, according to the photographs she was. We, her sons, never recognised beauty (or what I now, as a man, think of as beauty) in her. We were too young, too close to her. We loved the smell of her, especially when she wore furs, but the fact that she was a beautiful woman entirely escaped our understanding. What we did understand, however, from the moment we could read and converse and were taken travelling, was the difference between our mother's background and culture and our father's background and culture. Our father was French, the son of a colonel in the French army who was in turn the son of a colonel in the French army, and so on. His side of the family won so many medals, you could start a medal shop in the Rue des Saints Pères with them. Anyway, we are descended from a line of brave men. (The ribbon attached to medals is of a quality that I find very pleasing to handle: ribbed, silken and heavy. My father's hands have the feel of medal ribbon, wrinkled and silky.)

Our mother was English. She was born Emily Tregowan, the daughter of a self-educated Cornishman who made a respectable name in publishing. Though she spent almost all her married life in France, she never, I think, immersed herself in it, so that you could always perceive her Englishness sticking out like a flower too tall for the arrangement it's set in. And we, sent to an English boarding school, taken on visits to our Cornish grandfather in blustery summers, spent our childhood trying to decide what we were. At our boarding school, we were known as the Frog Twins. In Paris, neighbours referred to us as 'les gosses Anglais'. We preferred Paris to boarding school, as any boy would, but we liked the wildness of Cornwall. We knew that our father and all his ancestors had been brave, but Cornwall seemed to tell us that our mother and all hers had been wild, and we were inclined to prefer wildness to bravery. We are twins. We are now forty-two and both of us have lived, married and worked in France only. We never visit England, except occasionally on business, so time, you might say, has decided what we are: we are French. Yet our mother, and Cornwall, and what we once recognised was wild in a world of tame things have never passed out of memory and never will.

I shall describe us, not as we are now, but as we were at the time when our mother died, and our father – five years younger than she was – decided very quickly to remarry. Our mother died on a January Sunday near to our fifteenth birthday. Our English headmaster summoned us to his smokey study to unfold this colossal tiding. He stood up behind his oak desk and stared at us over his pipe: sallow, dark-haired boys with a dusting of pimples, thin hands, legs thinner than the gym master would have liked, an identical tendency to glower. We glowered, however, out of eyes the colour of scabious flowers – an extraordinary feature in us that has conquered any number of women, and which, among the traits which made up her beauty, we inherited from our mother. The rest of us is, and was already at fifteen, recognisably our father's: his thick hair, his small limbs, his yellowy complexion.

The news, I suppose, travelled round the school in delicious whispers: 'the Frog Twins' mother just died!' Boys squirmed with horror and delight. But we were snatched away and put on trains and freezing steamers till we reached Paris and the house in the Avenue Foch and our blind father fumbling round it. Nobody wept. When told of the death, my brother had started to hiccup violently and he hiccuped for three or four days, waking and sleeping. I picked my spots and knew that I wasn't ready for what had happened; death was too adult for me. And our father? He tried to bear himself like the soldier he was. But he became clumsy: he spilt food down his expensive clothes, he dropped and broke things. He also began to burble bits of poetry to himself, a thing which was absolutely uncharacteristic of him. I don't know what poetry it was that he burbled (I was more familiar, at fifteen, with Keats and Shelley and Tennyson than with Victor Hugo or Rimbaud) but I had the impression that he was muddling one poem with another and getting lots of words wrong. It was a very peculiar time: the hiccuping and the poetry and my own unreadiness for grief.

My brother, whose name I should have told you is Paul (mine is Jacques, a name I couldn't stand at the English school because even the masters nicknamed me 'Frère Jacques', just as if this wretched song was the only bit of French anyone English could be expected to understand), quite often *tried* to cry. I suppose he recognised, as I did, that we had not merely lost our mother, but the whole half of us that was Cornish and Anglo-Saxon. We remembered her stately walk in galoshes over the sandworms of Constantine Bay, her fondness for the sound of the seagulls. 'We may never see or hear another seagull,' my brother whispered one night, in search of tears that refused to come. 'Imagine poor Grandpa banging the seagull tin and remembering his dead daughter . . .' We waited anxiously for the first sob to break through. (Mourning only needs one; the others follow obediently.) But he couldn't cry.

He masturbated till he fell asleep, leaving me wide awake with the images of our mother he'd successfully summoned.

Grandpa's seagull tin was one that I have never forgotten. I can see my mother sitting on the wall at the end of his garden, smiling as Grandpa came out of the house. In an old washing bowl, Grandpa collected all the bread crusts and the leftover toast and stale cake. He came and stood in the middle of the lawn and banged loudly on the bottom of the tin with a wooden spoon. He'd done this twice a week for several years. Every seagull from Padstow to Trearnon seemed to know the signal. In seconds, even before he began to scatter the bread and cake, they'd come flapping in, hungry, unafraid, noisy with their cry which, even when it's near you, conjures distant oceans and faraway voyages. My mother sat on the wall and swang her legs and shrieked at them. Grandpa yelled, 'Go on! Go on!' as they came pecking and fighting. Paul and I ran up and down flapping our arms, as impressed by Grandpa as by a conjuror. We never knew Grandpa very well. Our father told us he was a reserved and self-disciplined man. But this is how I always remember him: surrounded by the seagulls, by the chaos he had caused.

We didn't go back to our English school after the funeral. We wondered if we would be sent back at all. Nobody said what was being planned for us. Our father stayed in his room, listening to the radio. Army friends called and the wives of army friends, who sometimes took him out for walks. He had an old manservant we called Blochot (I don't know whether Blochot was his real name, or just some family invention) who did for him all the things he couldn't do for himself. He seldom sent for us or wanted to be with us. In fact, he seemed to have forgotten us. We had one or two friends in the neighbourhood and we saw more of the parents of these friends than we did of our father. We spent weekends in the country with them. We went riding in the Bois. Now and again, we'd be taken to a meal in a restaurant.

The rest of the time we were in our room at the top of the house, reading the 'dirtiest' books you could get hold of at that time: *The Thousand and One Nights*, the *Rubaiyat of Omar Khayyam*, soothing colossal, inarticulate yearnings with solitary orgasms in crumpled handkerchiefs. As my life has gone on, it has occasionally hurt me — yes, *hurt* me — that I have known so little about my brother's sexuality. He has married two vain women in quick succession and kept his life with them secret from me. I remember the months in the room at the top of the house in the Avenue Foch, when every stirring of his penis and of mine was part of our shared grief, our shared confusion, our shared existence. And I remember of course the night of our father's second wedding, the night we decided to grow up. We parted soon after that. Now we meet for dinner and our wives bicker about the price of clothes. If I dared to ask Paul about his cock, he would get up and storm out of the restaurant.

It must have been in the spring that Pierrette arrived. She was a penniless person from a bourgeois family in Bourges. She had studied philosophy at the Sorbonne. She spoke a little very bad English. She didn't seem to know what to do with her philosophy degree except teach. She came to our house on a four-month contract to coach us until the end of the school year, at which time our father would decide what to do with us – send us back to our English school or to some new school in France. Nowadays, of course, an arrangement like this would never apply. In the event of the death of a parent, a child might expect a week off school and it would then be deemed 'in his best interests' to send him back to endure the gleeful pity of his friends. We were lucky, then, I dare say. We were allowed to stay in Paris – and at home. We forgot the cold English school.

Pierrette was twenty-three. Our father at that time must have been forty-two – the age we are now. Paul and I thought the name Pierrette was terrible. We couldn't imagine that anyone with a name like Pierrette could teach us anything at all. 'We'll teach her!' my brother crowed, 'we'll just speak English and confuse her and tell her the wrong meanings of words.'

She was a neat woman, very much a woman at twenty-three and not a girl. She spoke precisely and ate tidily. Her belongings were sparse and plain. She had a white, intelligent face and wispy, rather colourless hair. Her eyes were black and small and she had a black mole on her upper lip. Her hands were also white and neat and ringless. She wore tweed skirts and plain jerseys and her winter coat was ugly and unfashionable. 'Politeness!' growled our father from the depths of his favourite armchair, 'if you boys are not polite to this woman, there will be no summer for you!' No summer? Simultaneously, our minds flew to the seagulls and our mother on the wall. Of course there would be 'no summer', whether or not we decided to be polite. Summer as we had experienced it could no longer exist.

It never occurred to us, until we saw it happen, that Pierrette would fall in love with our father, and he, supposedly, with her. We thought Pierrette was just an episode in our lives, quickly gone and forgotten, like German measles. She was unsuitable as our teacher because she knew little Latin and her maths were second rate. She adored Pascal. She rubbed our noses in the Pensées of Pascal. All I can remember about Pierrette's lessons is Pascal: 'Jésus dans l'ennui . . .'

Her arrival coincided more or less with Blochot's illness. Blochot had glandular fever and though he struggled on, doing chores for our father, he was weak and silent and had to be encouraged to stay in bed. We tried to take his place, helping with tie-pins and bootlaces, searching for objects lost, tuning the radio, reading out wine labels, dialling telephone numbers. But I suppose we were clumsy and idle and impatient. Our father couldn't bear the way we did things. He used to push us away and whimper with frustration. And into the gap left by Blochot's glandular fever and our adolescent incompetence slipped Pierrette. Her careful hands and her quiet voice must have begun to press like a comforting little weight on father's sightlessness, reassuring him that life and order still existed, reminding him that only one woman had died, not the whole of womankind.

I can say this now. I am able to understand, now, how people may recover from tragedy. At fifteen, I couldn't understand. From the day when I walked into the first-floor drawing-room and saw my father reach out fumblingly for Pierrette, gathering her head in one hand and pressing her bottom towards him with the other, I understood only one thing: betrayal. I stood and stared. Pierrette saw me, but didn't pull away. Her face was pink with embarrassment and excitement. Her upper lip with its blemish of a mole was quivering out my father's christian name, his face was puckered, searching for those quivering lips. They kissed. My father's hand hitched up Pierrette's skirt and began scrabbling for the flesh above the stocking top. Pierrette turned to see if I was still there. I ran away.

Paul said he knew how to put an end to it. We lay in bed and planned how we would tell father that Pierrette was cross-eyed and horse-toothed and that her stocking seams were always crooked. We would also remind him of his military name and reputation, of our mother's beautiful laughter . . . As the traffic ceased and we half slept, my brother murmured, 'Perhaps there's nothing serious in it. Perhaps he'll just fuck her and she'll leave.' But I had seen the frantic hands, the searching lips; these seemed betrayal enough. 'He's got no loyalty,' I whispered, 'for all that he's a military man.'

I stole Pierrette's leatherbound edition of Pascal. I took it to the Quai St Michel and sold it. With the few francs I got for it, I bought roses and a pewter vase and lugged these to my mother's grave. In this futile action, I found some relief from my own incomprehension. Pierrette began to fret about the lost Pascal and the more she fretted the more I felt triumphant. But from this time on, we knew that something irreversible was growing between Pierrette and our father. Not caring what we thought, he'd come tapping up to the top floor where we had our so-called lessons and ask her to come down to him, 'to help me answer some letters', or to continue the mighty task he had invented for her – the re-cataloguing of his military history library. She would set us an essay to write, or some research to do and not return to us that day.

We'd tiptoe to our father's study, carrying our shoes. Pierrette and my father would be talking in whispers. We'd press our ears to the door. Very often, they seemed only to be talking about books. We'd stay hunched by the door till our feet grew numb, and they would simply talk on and on, quietly, intimately, like people who have loved each other for years.

One night, we saw Pierrette go to our father's room. We crept to his door, but all we could hear was laughter. Paul hated this. He went very white and led me away. 'I'm going to put a turd in her bed,' he announced, as we crept along the passage. I felt frightened: frightened by change which is final and irrevocable, frightened by the whiteness of my brother's face. We went to the bathroom. I sat on the bath edge and rocked to and fro to calm my fear and Paul sat on the lavatory, straining to produce the offensive offering he would stick between Pierrette's sheets. But my fear wouldn't go and Paul's bowels wouldn't move. *Status quo* . . . I repeated over and over, *status quo*.

One part of me wanted to be back at school. At least in England, in that jungle of rule and counter-rule, we would be away from what was happening. We could grieve for our mother in her own country and have no part in this hothouse betrayal. But we knew we wouldn't be sent back until the autumn. Easter came, and Pierrette went home to her family in Bourges. We cheered up. Blochot recovered and started work again. We were given money for spring clothes. Our father resumed his walks with the army wives. Pierrette was not mentioned. We were invited to an uncle's house in the Loire valley. We left Paris with relief and our father stayed behind. When we returned, Pierrette was back.

*

We had never done any of the things we'd planned. We'd never tried to pretend to the blind man that Pierrette had flat feet or buck teeth. I had sold her Pensées, but she never knew it was me. At lessons, we were sulky and uncooperative and made snobby remarks about the bourgeois of Bourges, but to our father we were polite in a cold kind of way. He didn't seem to notice any change in us.

It was an extraordinary spring in Paris. The railings outside our house were warm; the magnolia tree pushed out its showy blooms into an air of utter stillness. We strode around in our new clothes and thought of the long summer. At the end of May, we were summoned to the drawing room and told by our father that he was going to marry Pierrette. Pierrette wasn't there. He had granted us this courtesy; he knew we would require an explanation. 'Never doubt,' he said, 'my love for your mother. She was a remarkable woman and I trust that you may be so fortunate as to have inherited some of her qualities. But when you grow up and become men, you will, I hope, understand that a man of my years cannot content himself with a celibate life. It is not in a man's nature. And Pierrette and I have found in each other an affinity I never thought I would be lucky enough to feel. I may as well admit to you that, much as I admired your mother, we were never

54

sexually compatible and our marriage was not successful from this point of view.'

Tears began to stream down Paul's face. I remembered, grimly, how hard he had tried to cry after our mother's death. I pinched his arm. I didn't think this was a moment for weakness.

'May we go now, father?' I asked.

'Go? Aren't you going to offer me your congratulations?'

Paul made a choking sound. I tugged him towards the door. My father's head jerked up.

'Is one of you crying?'

'No,' I stammered, 'Paul's got a cold. Congratulations, father.'

I got Paul up to our room, where he lay on the bed and sobbed and shook. I stole a bottle of brandy from Blochot's pantry, took this upstairs and tried to dribble some into Paul's runny mouth. In the end, he gulped quite a lot of brandy down, I covered him with my eiderdown and he went to sleep, still shuddering.

We were fifteen by then, not obviously tall or strong or handsome, yet, being twins, we enjoyed attention from people which, singly, neither of us would have earned. It was as if the two of us equalled one very striking person. We are not identical, yet have a strong resemblance. At forty-two, I know that I look older than Paul. At fifteen, our experience of life had been in every way identical and neither we, nor people we met, could separate us out. And over the question of father's marriage, we acted of course as one. We offered Pierrette glacial felicitations; we told our snobby Parisian friends that father was marrying 'an ugly bourgeoise from Bourges'; we fuelled Blochot's sense of something done too hastily by reminding him constantly of all the years we had been 'one family', with our mother, nostrils flared as if breathing the air of the sea, in her place at the helm. We did everything we could, in fact, to wreck the coming marriage, by insinuation, by sulking, by discourtesy, and by downright lies. Yet we knew it would happen. One morning we'd wake up and that would be the day, and after it what? After it, *what*? We asked each other that question very often: what happens when it's over?

It was a July wedding, held in Paris and not in Bourges in deference to our father's blindness and Pierrette's sense of grandeur. The reception took place in the drawing room of our house. Pierrette wore a white coat and skirt and an ugly white velvet hat which made her look like a rich American child. The Bourges relations clearly envied her her new life and wondered (but did not ask) how a philosophy degree had won her a soldier. My father pinned his medals onto his dress uniform. His blind person's gestures were already the gestures of an old man, yet on that day Blochot had helped him to look resplendent and brave, which, in his way, he was.

Paul and I had been bought identical grey suits. All suits, in those days, seemed to be grey and we wore them obediently, not proudly. The buttonhole carnations we had been given we decided not to pin on. At one time, Paul had wanted to make us black armbands, but these, I calculated, would have been more shocking and insulting in their way than any of the punishments we had thought up. So I suggested instead that we simply get drunk and try to pretend that nothing mattered – life, death, blindness, war, bereavement, marriage, crooked stocking seams – nothing signified. We had seen it all.

*

The honeymoon was to be in a house on the Côte d'Azur, leant by some uncle or rich godfather. But our father knew he would find the reception tiring, so it was decided that he and Pierrette would take the Paris-to-Nice sleeper the following evening. The wedding night would be spent in our house.

By eight or nine, all the reception guests, there since two, had trickled away into the stifling evening. My father stood on one of the balconies, jerking his head in the direction of the sun tumbling straight down behind the Avenue de la Grande Armée, his hand clasping his new bride to him, his body in its dress uniform very straight and proud. We, lolling on sofas, slightly bilious from the quantity of champagne we had drunk, stared at their backs in silent contempt. 'It's as if,' Paul whispered, 'mother had never existed.' Pierrette turned and stared at us, her skin blotchy with excitement and alcohol. 'I suggest,' she said, in a voice of new authority, 'that you boys get yourselves some supper and go to bed.'

Father didn't move. We were dismissed. We slipped sullenly away, carrying our jackets and ties that we had taken off. We climbed the stairs to our room. We didn't speak. What had invaded us, at precisely the same moment, was a boredom so colossal, so heavy and unyielding that neither of us could utter. Life wasn't tragic after all; it was dull. In the south of England, an old man banged a washing bowl and greedy gulls began to circle, but there was no magic in it, only boring reflex and tearing, ugly beaks. All was predictable and ignoble and stupid. The roses in the pewter vase had long ago wilted and turned brown. Some old scavenging woman with her savings in a shoebox had stolen the vase, just as the leatherbound copy of Pascal had been stolen. Nothing signified – no gesture or act or artefact or idea. Jésus dans l'ennui . . . No one had redeemed man from his eternal mediocrity.

We lay in silence for several hours, sprawled on our beds, dozing now and then. Darkness came. In the dark, the sounds of the street below seemed to grow louder. Cars roared. Lights came glimmering on.

'I'm going down,' Paul announced suddenly, 'to buy us a woman.'

We stared at each other. In that instant, boredom had disappeared, belief in magic returned. To find it, we only had to reach out and dip into the darkness.

'It's expensive,' I said nonchalantly.

'We'll get a cheap one.'

'How would one tell . . .?'

'Which are the cheap ones? The old ones.'

'Let's not get an old one.'

'How much have you got?'

The thought slipped into my mind, if I hadn't bought the pewter vase . . . I banished it. 'About three thousand francs,' I said.

'I've got more than that,' said Paul. 'We should be alright. We can probably afford one who looks young in the dark.'

'What about the room?' I said.

'The room?'

'Well, look at it. She'll be able to tell it's just a boys' room.'

'Yes. Well, let's tidy it at least.'

Urgently then we bundled away the litter of clothes into the wardrobes, put the *Thousand and One Nights* back into its *Jock of the Bushveld* dustjacket, and, silently as we could, moved the two beds together and covered them with the satin eiderdowns. Finally, Paul hunted in his chest of drawers for a red paisley silk scarf – a present from our English grandfather – which he draped round the central parchment lampshade. The room was transformed by the light, reddened, ready.

'Well . . .' I said.

'Why don't you go down?' said Paul.

'Me?'

'Yes. You're taller.'

'No, I'm not. We're the same.'

'You look older.'

So it was that around midnight I found myself with seven thousand francs in my pocket, carrying my shoes, creeping silently down past our father's room where the lights were turned out, past the drawing room where the one hundred guests had eaten salmon, down into the hall which had been filled with flowers and out at last into the street.

The night was colder than I had expected. I was glad I'd done up my tie and put my jacket on. I was nervous, yet I felt light with my own extraordinary purpose. My whole life shadowed me as I walked; the shadow was obedient and vast.

We knew where the whores congregated. The Avenue Foch was the rather verdant beat of a cavalcade of spikey-eyed women. In gateways and on corners, they stood and waited. Cars drew up. They got in, in ones and twos. Hunched up men steered them away down side streets. I had often passed these furtive stoppings, noted the quick exchange of words, the clacking heels being hurried over the cobbles, little wisps of laughter or anger trailing off into the night.

I felt tiny. The city hummed, like a dome, round me. I walked very slowly, hearing each footstep. The night was superb. I pitied my father who would never see it – the Arc de Triomphe on its hill of light, the glistening foliage of gardens and entrances, a cluster of stars above the tall-shouldered houses . . . I thought of Paul, waiting on the satin eiderdowns and grinned. I have never admired my brother as ardently as I did that night. I admired him firstly for his daring and secondly for the cowardice which had tempered it and which allowed me to be here in the street. I truly loved him.

The two women I stopped at, hesitating, my hand clutching the money in my pocket, looked at me first with the disdain of giraffes, then, seeing me planted in front of them, speechless but earnest, they smiled and made almost identical movements of their hips, shifting weight from one long leg to the other. The thought whizzed through me: will women always be taller than me? I cleared my throat. 'I didn't know . . .' I began, 'whether one of you might like to . . . come along to my house. I mean, just for half an hour or something . . .'

The women looked at each other and grinned, looked back at me, grinned again.

'Which one of us did you have in mind?'

I remembered Paul's knowing statement: the oldest are the cheapest. Neither of these women seemed particularly old, nor particularly young. I couldn't have told whether they were twenty-five or forty. They were just women – available women. I stared up at them, trying to guess which of them might be the cheapest, but I simply couldn't tell. Nor, I realised, did I want to offend either of them by choosing one and rejecting the other.

'I don't really mind,' I said, 'I mean, I don't mind at all. The thing is that I've got seven thousand francs . . .'

Again, they looked at each other and grinned. One of them pulled a silky shawl round her shoulders, touched my chin lightly and tenderly and began to walk away. I watched her go with a feeling of dismay. She suddenly seemed perfect: long, dark hair, swinging as she walked, a fleshy bottom encased in a tight skirt that shimmered. I wanted to call her back, but I felt a gentle hand on my arm and forced myself to look more closely at the woman who was to be ours. She had red hair and a wide smile. She wore a lacy blouse over bunched up, milky breasts. On her upper lip was the dark blotch of a mole.

*

'Somebody like flowers in this house?' she said, seeing the banked arrangements that filled the hall.

'Ssh,' I whispered, 'my father's in bed. He had his wedding today.'

She began to laugh, put a fist up to stifle it. From the fist hung a little ornate velvet purse with an amber clasp. Soon, all my savings and Paul's would be inside this purse.

A light was on under my father's door now as we passed it. I imagined him hearing our footsteps, feeling his way to the door and opening it – and seeing nothing of course. To live with a blind man is to have the power of invisibility. We

59

hurried on up, me leading, not daring to look behind me. Was the red-haired woman old? How would she seem to Paul in the paisley lamplight? Would he mind the mole on her lip? Old women don't have red hair or high breasts, do they? I felt absolutely responsible to Paul for my choice. My own daring had only been in recognition of his. We had a perfect sense, in those days, of what each of us owed to the other. Over the years, this sense has clouded, disappeared.

'Here we are,' I said, quietly opening the door to our room. Paul, who had been sitting on the edge of the bed, trying not to crumple the eiderdown, stood up stiffly.

'Oh, good evening . . .' he said.

I put my hand on the woman's arm and led her forward. The skin of her arm was freckled and soft. Her hair, I saw now, was a marvellous colour and very clean.

'This is my twin brother, Paul,' I said apologetically. 'I wonder if you could tell us your name?'

'Oh yes. Bettina. All nations can pronounce 'Bettina'.'

'Oh. All nations, eh?'

'I think it's a terrific name,' said Paul.

Bettina was smiling. I felt relieved. I hadn't dared to tell her there would be two of us. She crossed to the bed, sat down and looked up at us.

'Money first,' she said, opening the velvet purse. 'Five thousand each. I like to get this part of it over. Then we can enjoy ourselves, eh?'

I produced the seven thousand. 'This is really all we've got . . .' I began, but Paul, without any hesitation, had tugged out the gold cufflinks given to him that very morning by our father and Pierrette (an identical pair to me) to mark their wedding day.

'I'd be honoured,' he said in a speechy voice, 'if you would accept these. They are worth considerably more than the three thousand owing to you.'

Bettina took them, inspected them for the gold hallmark, dropped them and the crumpled notes I had given her into the purse. She laid the purse down, kicked off her shoes and began to unroll her stockings.

I sat down. I was shaking, not with sexual excitement, but with a sense of absolute strangeness. I thought, the walk out into the night, everything from that moment is a dream and I shall wake up in the morning and life will be precisely as it was, with only the *Thousand and One Nights* within my reach. There will have been no scarf on the lampshade, no act of daring and maturity . . . I blinked, rubbed my eyes, felt thirsty, stared at Paul, who was unbuttoning his trousers. I longed for a cool drink of milk or lemonade, but I had the notion that time was sliding away from me immeasurably fast; yes, life itself was slipping, altering, as Paul stepped out of his trousers, nervously fingering his penis, already erect, and I had to stay and be part of it, or miss it for ever.

I sat on the bed and watched as Bettina arrayed for us on the satin eiderdowns a body of such white voluptuousness its form has stayed huddled in memory all my life and through all my loving. Flesh has never again seemed in itself so magnificent a thing, so utterly and uncontrollably inviting. All strangeness, all fear vanished. Paul parted Bettina's legs, and we glimpsed for the first time in our lives the glistening dark channel that puerile imagination never imagines perfectly enough, the deep and private walls of ripeness, where the boy deluges his fountain of dreams.

I don't remember taking off my clothes, yet I was naked on the bed, my hand on Paul's buttocks. The motions his body made were tender, unembarrassed, as touching as an animal. His body shone. I was choked by his achievement, his beauty. My head on Bettina's scented hair, I pressed myself to the one body that hers and Paul's had become, rocked as they rocked, felt myself move as Paul moved through waves of mounting ecstasy. 'It's superb!' Paul trumpeted as he moved and I moved faster and faster, 'it's superb, Jacques!'

*

I don't know whether it was my father's decision or Pierrette's to separate Paul's life from mine, but this, at the end of the summer, was what happened. We were taken away from our English school for good and sent to different boarding schools in France. I have never been able to understand the reasoning behind this decision and can only guess at it: if we missed each other enough, we would cease to miss our mother, and thus to talk of her.

The odd thing is that ever since that time, I have, all my life, missed them both. Paul's life has taken such a different course from my own that I have long ago lost him as a brother. The man he is, the man I meet at restaurants with our wives, is at best an acquaintance – an acquaintance I don't even like very much.

During periods of anxiety or depression, and only then, do these two ghosts visit me as once they were: Paul making first love to Bettina under the paisley light; my mother sitting on a wall in Cornwall and yelling at the gulls.

My Wife Is a White Russian

I'm a financier. I have financial assets, world-wide. I'm in nickel and pig-iron and gold and diamonds. I like the sound of all these words. They have an edge, I think. The glitter of saying them sometimes gives me an erection.

I'm saying them now, in this French restaurant, where the tablecloths and the table napkins are blue linen, where they serve sea-food on platters of seaweed and crushed ice. It's noisy at lunchtime. It's May and the sun shines in London, through the open restaurant windows. Opposite me, the two young Australians blink as they wait (so damned courteous, and she has freckles like a child) for me to stutter out my hard-word list, to manipulate tongue and memory so that the sound inside me forms just behind my lips and explodes with extraordinary force above my oysters.

Diamonds!

But then I feel a soft, perfumed dabbing at my face. I turn away from the Australians and there she is. My wife. She is smiling as she wipes me. Her gold bracelets rattle. She is smiling at me. Her lips are astonishing, the colour of claret. I've been wanting to ask her for some time: 'Why are your lips this terrible dark colour these days? Is it a lipstick you put on?'

Still smiling at me, she's talking to the Australians with her odd accent: 'He's able to enjoy the pleasures of life once more, thank God. For a long time afterwards, I couldn't take him out. Terrible. We couldn't do one single thing, you know. But now . . . He enjoys his wine again.'

The dabbing stops. To the nurse I tried to say when I felt a movement begin: 'Teach me how to wipe my arse. I cannot let my wife do this because she doesn't love me. If she loved me, she probably wouldn't mind wiping my arse and I wouldn't mind her wiping my arse. But she doesn't love me.'

The Australian man is talking now. I let my hand go up and take hold of my big-bowled wine glass into which a waiter has poured the expensive Chablis my wife likes to drink when she eats fish. Slowly, I guide the glass across the deadweight distance between the table and my mouth. I say 'deadweight' because the spaces between all my limbs and the surfaces of tangible things have become mighty. To walk is to wade in waist-high water. And to lift this wine glass . . . 'Help me,' I want to say to her, 'just this once. Just this once.'

'Heck,' says the Australian man, 'we honestly thought he'd made a pretty positive recovery.' His wife, with blue eyes the colour of the napkins, is watching my struggles with the glass. She licks her fine line of a mouth, sensing, I suppose, my longing to taste the wine. The nurse used to stand behind me, guiding the feeding cup in my hand. I never explained to her that the weight of gravity had mysteriously increased. Yet often, as I drank from the feeding cup, I used to imagine myself prancing on the moon.

'Oh this is a very positive recovery,' says my wife. 'There's very little he can't do now. He enjoys the ballet, you know, and the opera. People at Covent Garden and the better kind of place are very considerate. We don't go to the cinema because there you have a very inconsiderate type of person. Don't you agree? So riff-raffy? Don't you agree?'

The Australian wife hasn't listened to a word. The Australian wife puts out a lean freckled arm and I watch it come towards me, astounded as usual these days by the speed with which other people can move parts of their bodies. But the arm, six inches from my hand holding the glass, suddenly stops. 'Don't help him!' snaps my wife. The napkin-blue eyes are lowered. The arm is folded away.

Heads turn in the restaurant. I suppose her voice has carried its inevitable echo round the room where we sit: 'Don't help him! Don't help him! But now that I have an audience, the glass begins to jolt, the wine splashing up and down the sides of the bowl. I smile. My smile widens as I watch the Chablis begin to slop onto the starched blue cloth. *Waste!* She of all people understands the exquisite luxury of waste. Yet she snatches the glass out of my hand and sets it down by her own. She snaps her fingers and a young beanstick of a waiter arrives. He spreads out a fresh blue napkin where I have spilt my wine. My wife smiles her claret smile. She sucks an oyster into her dark mouth.

The Australian man is, I was told, the manager of the Toomin Valley Nickel Consortium. The Australian man is here to discuss expansion, supposedly with me, unaware until he met me this lunchtime that, despite the pleasing cadences of the words, I'm unable to say 'Toomin Valley Nickel Consortium'. I can say 'nickel'. My tongue lashes around in my throat to form the click that comes in the middle of the word. Then out it spills. Nickel! In my mind, oddly enough, the word 'nickel' is the exact greyish-white colour of an oyster. But 'consortium' is too difficult for me. I know my limitations.

My wife is talking again: 'I've always loved the ballet, you see. This is my only happy memory of Russia – the wonderful classical ballet. A little magic. Don't you think? I would never want to be without this kind of magic, would you? Do you have the first-rate ballet companies in Australia? You do? Well, that's good. *Giselle* of course. That's the best one. Don't you think? The dead girl. Don't you think? Wonderful.'

We met on a pavement. I believe it was in the Avenue Matignon but it could have been in the Avenue Montaigne. I often get these muddled. It was in Paris, anyway. Early summer, as it is now. Chestnut candle blooms blown along the gutters. I waited to get into the taxi she was leaving. But I didn't get into it. I followed her. In a bar, she told me she was very poor. Her father drove the taxi I had almost hired. She spoke no English then, only French with a heavy Russian accent. I was just starting to be a financier at that time, but already I was quite rich, rich by her standards – she who had been used to life in post-war Russia. My hotel room was rather grand. She said in her odd French: 'I'll fuck for money.'

I gave her fifty francs. I suppose it wasn't much, not as much as she'd hoped for, a poor rate of exchange for the white, white body that rode astride me, head thrown back, breasts bouncing. She sat at the dressing table in the hotel room. She smoked my American cigarettes. More than anything, I wanted to brush her gold hair, brush it smooth and hold it against my face. But I didn't ask her if I could do this. I believe I was afraid she would say: 'You can do it for money.'

The thin waiter is clearing away our oyster platters. I've eaten only three of my oysters, yet I let my plate go. She pretends not to notice how slow I've been with the oysters. And my glass of wine still stands by hers, untasted. Yet she's drinking quite fast. I hear her order a second bottle. The Australian man says: 'First-rate choice, if I may say. We like Chably.' I raise my left arm and touch her elbow, nodding at the wine. Without looking at me, she puts my glass down in front of me. The Australian wife stares at it. Neither she nor I dare to touch it.

My wife is explaining to the Australians what they are about to eat, as if they were children: 'I think you will like the turbot very much. *Turbot poché hollandaise.* They cook it very finely. And the hollandaise sauce, you know this of course? Very difficult to achieve, lightness of this sauce. But here they do it very well. And the scallops in saffron. Again a very light sauce. Excellent texture. Just a little cream added. And fresh scallops naturally. We never go to any restaurant where the food is frozen. So I think you will like these dishes you have chosen very much . . .'

We have separate rooms. Long before my illness, when I began to look (yet hardly to feel) old, she demanded her privacy. This was how she put it: she wanted to be private. The bedroom we used to share and which is now hers is very large. The walls are silk. She said: 'There's no sense in being rich and then cooped up together in one room.' Obediently, I moved out. She wouldn't let me have the guest room, which is also big. I have what we call 'the little room', which I always used to think of as a child's room. In her 'privacy' I expect she smiles: 'the child's room is completely right for him. He's a helpless baby!' Yet she's not a private person. She likes to go out four or five nights a week, returning at two or three in the morning, sometimes with friends, sitting and drinking brandy. Sometimes they play music. Elton John. She has a lover (I don't know his name) who sends her lilies.

I'm trying to remember the Toomin Valley. I believe it's an immense desert of a place, inhabited by no one and nothing except the mining machinery and the Nickel Consortium employees, whose clusters of houses I ordered to be whitewashed to hide the cheap grey building blocks. The windows of the houses are small, to keep out the sun. In the back yards are spindly eucalyptus trees, blown by the scorching winds. I want to ask the Australian wife: 'Did you have freckles before you went to live in the Toomin Valley, and does some wandering prima ballerina dance *Giselle* on the gritty escarpment above the mine?'

My scallops arrive, saffron yellow and orange in the blue and white dish – the colours of a childhood summer. The flesh of a scallop is firm yet soft, the texture of a woman's thigh (when she is young, of course; before the skin hardens and the flesh bags out). A forkful of scallop is immeasurably easier to lift than the glass of wine, and the Australian wife (why don't I know either of their names?) smiles at me approvingly as I lift the succulent parcel of food to my mouth and chew it without dribbling. My wife, too, is watching, ready with the little scented handkerchief, yet talking as she eats, talking of Australia as the second bottle of Chablis arrives and she tastes it hurriedly, with a curt nod to the thin waiter. I exist only in the corner of her eye, at its inmost edge, where the vulnerable triangle of red flesh is startling.

'Of course I've often tried to tell Hubert' (she pronounces my name 'Eieu-bert', trying and failing with what she recognises as the upper class 'h') 'that it's very unfair to expect people like you to live in some out-of-the-way place. I was brought up in a village, you see, and I know that an out-of-the-way village is so dead. No culture. The same in Toomin, no? Absolutely no culture at all. Everybody dead.'

The Australian wife looks – seemingly for the first time – straight at my wife. 'We're outdoor people,' she says.

I remember now. A river used to flow through the Toomin Valley. Torrential in the rainy season, they said. It dried up in the early forties. One or two sparse willows remain, grey testimony to the long-ago existence of water-rich soil. I imagine the young Australian couple, brown as chestnuts, swimming in the Toomin River, resting on its gentle banks with their fingers touching, a little loving nest of bone. There is no river. Yet when they look at each other, almost furtively under my vacant gaze, I recognise the look. The look says: 'These moments with strangers are nothing. Into our private moments together – only there – is crammed all that we ask of a life.'

'Yes, we're outdoor folk.' The Australian man is smiling. 'You can play tennis most of the year round at Toomin. I'm President of the Tennis Club. And we have our own pool now.'

I don't remember these things: tennis courts and swimming pools.

'Well, of course you have the climate for this.' My wife is signalling our waiter to bring her Perrier water. 'And it's something to do, isn't it? Perhaps, when the new expansions of the company are made, a concert hall could be built for you, or a theatre?'

'A theatre!' The Australian wife's mouth opens to reveal perfect, freshly peeled teeth and a laugh escapes. She blushes. My wife's dark lips are puckered into a sneer. But the Australian man is laughing too – a rich laugh you might easily remember on the other side of the world – and slapping his thigh. 'A theatre! What about that, ay!'

She wanted, she said as she smoked my American cigarettes, to see *Don Giovanni*. Since leaving Russia with her French mother and her Russian father, no one had ever taken her to the opera. She had seen the posters advertising *Don Giovanni* and asked her father to buy her a ticket. He had shouted at her: 'Remember whose child you are! Do you imagine taxi drivers can afford seats at the Opéra?'

'Take me to see *Don Giovanni*,' she said, 'and then I will fuck for nothing.'

I've never really appreciated the opera. The Don was fat. It was difficult imagining so many women wanting to lie with this fat man. Yet afterwards, she leant over and put her head on my shoulder and wept. Nothing, she told me, had ever moved her so much, nothing in her life had touched the core of her being as this had done, this production of *Don Giovanni*. 'If only,' she said, 'I had money as you have money, then I would go to hear music all the time and see the classical ballet and learn from these what is life.'

The scallops are good. She never learned what is life. I feel emboldened by the food. I put my hand to my glass, heavier than ever now because the waiter has filled it up. The sun shines on my wine and on my hand blotched (splattered, it seems) with the oddly repulsive stains of old age. For a second, I see my hand and the wine glass as a still-life. But then I lift the glass. The Australian wife lowers her eyes. My wife for a moment is silent. I drink. I smile at the Australian wife because I know she wants to applaud.

I'm talking. The words are like stones, weighing down my lower jaw. Nickel. I'm trying to tell the Australian man that I dream about the nickel mine. In my dreams, the Australian miners drag carts loaded with threepenny bits. I run my hands through the coins as through a sack of wheat, and the touch of them is pleasurable and perfect. I also want to say to the Australian man: 'I hope you're happy in your work. When I was in control, I visited all my mines and all my subsidiaries at least once a year. Even in South Africa, I made sure a living wage was paid. I said to the men underground, I hope you're happy in your work.'

But now I have a manager, a head manager to manage all the other managers, including this one from the Toomin Valley. I am trundled out in my chair to meet them when they come here to discuss redundancy or expansion. My wife and I give them lunch in a restaurant. They remind me that I still have an empire to rule, if I was capable, if my heart had not faltered, if indeed my life had been different since the night of *Don Giovanni*.

When I stopped paying her to sleep with me, her father came to see me. He held his cap in his hands. 'We're hoping for a marriage,' he said. And what more could I have given – what *less* to the body I had begun to need so terribly? The white and gold of her, I thought, will ornament my life.

Yet now I never touch her. The white and the gold of her lies only in the lilies they send, the unknown lovers she finds in the night, while I lie in the child's room and dream of the nickel mines. My heart is scorched dry like the dry hills of the Toomin Valley. I am punished for my need of her while her life stalks my silence: the white of her, the gold of her – the white of Dior, the gold of Cartier. Why did she never love me? In my dreams, too, the answer comes from deep underground: it's the hardness of my words.

Dinner For One

He said: 'I'll take you out. We'll go to Partridge's, have something special.' She took off her glasses and looked at him doubtfully.

'I don't know, Henry. I don't know that we want to make a fuss about it.'

'Well, it's up to you.'

'Why is it?'

'Why is it what?'

'Up to me?'

She bewildered him. For years she had bewildered him. 'It's your choice, Lal; that's all I meant. It's your choice – whether we go out or not.'

She sighed. 'I just thought . . .'

'What?'

'I just thought it might be better simply to treat it like any other day.'

'It's not "any other day".'

'No.'

'But it's your decision. You're the one who makes these decisions. So you let me know if you want to go and I'll ring up and book a table.'

He walked away from her, sat down in his worn red armchair, fumbled for his glasses, found them and took up *The Times* crossword. She watched him, still holding her glasses in her hand. It's funny, she thought, that whenever we talk to each other, we take our glasses off. We blur each other out. I suppose we're afraid that if we see each other clearly – too clearly – communication between us will cease.

'Six across . . .' he murmured from the faded comfort of his chair, 'two words, four and three: "Facts of severing the line".'

'Anagram,' she whispered, 'I should think.'

Henry and Lal weren't what anyone expected. Separate from her, he seemed to belong. He belongs; she doesn't, was what people thought. You could pull old Henry's leg and raise that boisterous laugh of his, but with her you didn't know where you were. Quite ordinary remarks – things that everyone laughed at – seemed to worry her. But she never told you why: she just closed her eyes.

There had been so many friends at the beginning. Henry and Lal had belonged then. 'Isn't my wife the belle of the ball?' he used to say. And there were so many balls, once, to be belle of. The changes had stolen gradually into her; the changes had begun after Henry came home from the War, so that people often said: 'It was the War that changed her,' and even to her face: 'It was the War that changed you, Lal, wasn't it?'

But she didn't agree with them. 'The War changed everyone,' was all she'd say.

'It always seems . . .'

Henry looked up from the crossword. He was surprised Lal was still in the room. 'What, Lal?'

'Such a waste.'

'What does?'

'Going out. All that eating.'

'We can afford it, darling.'

'Oh, it isn't that.'

Henry took off his glasses. 'Well, I'm damned if I –'

'Look at our stomachs! Look at yours. So crammed with food you couldn't push any more in. And mine, a dreadful bulge.'

'Oh, Lal, for heaven's sake.'

'It's horrible to eat and eat. What's it for? Just to make us heavier and heavier till we die with all this weight.'

'You're not fat, Lal. I'm fat! I'm not ashamed of it.'

'Why.'

'Why what?'

'Why aren't you ashamed?'

'Because it's *my* life. I can be any shape I choose.'

No, she thought, that's wrong. I am haunted by the wrongness of things.

'Henry,' she said, 'I hate it –'

'What?'
'I hate it when –'

*

Larry Partridge was a popular man. 'We're so lucky,' ran the county's favourite saying, 'to have you so near us!' They didn't mean Larry himself (though they liked his silver-haired politeness), they meant his restaurant which, every night of the week except Tuesdays when it was closed, was packed with them.

'This part of the world was a culinary desert before you came, Larry,' they told him, 'but now we really are lucky. Partridge's is as good as anything in London and so much more reasonable.'

Of course they had been cautious – caution before ecstasy – because, glancing through the windows of the old run-down pub he had bought, they had noted that the old run-down walls were becoming resplendent in indigos and fruit-fool pinks and this had made them nudge each other: 'Well, you can tell what *he* is, duckie!'

Now Larry's tightly-clad buttocks circled their contented after-dinner smiles. He extended to each table a limp-handed greeting and waited for the superlatives to flood his ears like warm water. 'You're so imaginative with food, Larry!'

'The sauce on the quenelles was out of this world, Larry.'

'We've had a superb meal, Larry, really superb.'

*

Larry's parents still lived in Romford. He had moved them from their council flat to a detached house. However, Larry's father still called him Lawrence. Lawrence: to say the name to himself was to remind Larry of his father, was to make him shudder as if the thin shadow of the man – neat in his dark green suit and white shirt, ready for work, working all his life, never giving up his dull and hopeless work till one day he would die at it – passed between him and the sun.

For Larry, Lawrence was dead, buried hideously down in the greasy kitchens of the catering school. Lawrence, born in poverty, reared in repression, was the detritus from which Larry, in all his colourful glory, had sprung. He had sprung in 1964, the year he had met Edwin, and each year since then he had bloomed a little more.

'What can I say about Edwin?' Larry had asked his mother at the time, 'except that I love him.'

Oh, but they were not prepared for this kind of love, she told him. They had never thought that their own Lawrence, so popular with all the local girls . . . No, it had not once entered their minds and she really did think he should have given them some warning, some indication that he wasn't what they thought . . .

Larry left his parents' flat in Romford and moved into Edwin's flat in Fulham. Edwin found him a job in a local restaurant. Lawrence in Edwin's careful drawing room became Larry, became lover and loved.

All the past, like a dirty old bandage no longer needed, began to unwind and fall off; Larry was healed.

Edwin's money purchased the pub in 1972. One end of the large building was converted into a flat and the move from Fulham was made. A year later, Partridge's opened, each of its walls a reflection of Edwin's taste, Edwin's imaginative eye.

Larry moved with perfect ease and happiness about his steel kitchen, liking his own little kingdom the better because just outside it was a rich land that he shared with Edwin.

'I do it with love,' Larry sometimes said of his cooking. But the great golden weight of his love for Edwin he seldom talked of. It hung inside him, a burdensome treasure that he knew would never leave him.

Visitors to Partridge's never saw Edwin. Larry's nightly ritual of passing from table to table to receive his cupful of praise did not include him. He was glimpsed occasionally; there was talk of him, even questions to Larry.

'But it's all yours,' Edwin had said to Larry when the restaurant opened. 'My bit's done. Don't involve me any more. Then the success and the glory will really belong to you.'

And even the invitations that came – to the lunches and the county cocktail parties – Edwin would never accept. 'You're their celebrity, Larry. Why muddle them?'

Edwin was never jealous. 'I am quite free of it,' he once said to Larry. 'I simply do not feel it. Jealousy is the vainest – in all senses – of the emotions. You must learn to rid yourself of that before it works its decay.'

But Larry had known no human relationship in which jealousy had not been present – sometimes screamed out, sometimes unspoken, but always there to stain and spoil.

And he knew that his love for Edwin was a jealous, greedy love. He thought to himself: "Edwin is my life. How can I not be jealous of my own life?" Whenever Edwin went away, the weight inside him became a dead weight, immovable, full of pain.

When Edwin returned, he often wanted to run to him, discovering in his body a sudden miraculous lightness.

*

Daily, Larry watched Edwin for any sign of discontent. Three years younger than Larry his hair was still fair and thick. With an impatient gesture of his hand, he would push back the flopping hair several times in an hour.

Whenever he was angry or agitated, he would push back the hair almost constantly.

Larry dreaded his anger. Its occasional appearance in a man as contained and rational as Edwin was unsightly. Larry couldn't look at him. He would turn away, trembling inside.

But in the hundreds of times he had turned away like this over the years, there was not one time that he had not dreaded to turn round again, afraid suddenly that all the hubbub of Edwin's anger was nothing but an echo and that, unnoticed, Edwin had quietly slipped away and left him.

Edwin did little with his time. He gave to unimportant things the careful attention of his hands. He grew roses. He did occasional pen and ink drawings of old houses, which Larry collected and had framed.

He made an elegant coffee table out of glass and wood. He wrote a little poetry, always laughing at what he had written and throwing it away.

Money had bought Edwin a studied indolence. 'I'm really a rocking-chair man,' he once said to Larry. 'The little motions I can make are enough.'

Certainly, they were enough for Larry. He was quite content for Edwin to be just as he was – as long as he was always there.

*

Lal said: 'I've worked out that anagram.' Several moments had passed in silence. Henry had filled in two more clues in *The Times* crossword. Lal had walked to the study window and looked out at the bird table she festooned in winter with strings of nuts and pieces of coconut. The nuts were eaten, the coconut pecked dry: it was springtime.

Henry looked up. 'What was that you said, Lal?'

'Two words, four and three, "Facts of severing the line".'

'I've got that one, haven't I?'

'I don't know. It's "cast off" – anagram of "facts of".'

'Let me see, "cast off"? You're right, Lal. Good for you.'

Henry filled it in. Then he looked up at Lal standing by the window. 'Made up your mind yet, darling?'

Lal knew that he meant the dinner, knew that she had made up her mind. She didn't want to go out with Henry on that day.

A reward, she thought – a more fitting one for fifty years of marriage – should be to spend that evening alone, without him.

For the clear lines with which she encircled the petty wrong-nesses of her life became each time like the lines drawn by aeroplanes in a blue sky: they fuzzed and were dissipated and the spaces where they had been were filled up, so that only a moment later you couldn't see that they had been there. Life went on in the old way.

In the mass of years she kept drawing and redrawing lines, kept believing that things might change one day and she would rediscover something lost.

'I have made up my mind,' Lal said. 'I think we should go out as you suggested. It would be nice to go to Partridge's, don't you think?'

'Well, I do.'

'Only . . .'

'What?'

'It's a Tuesday. Larry shuts on a Tuesday.'

'Damn me! Never mind, we'll make it the Monday. Why not? We can toast the midnight. As they used to say in the army, always better to have the feast before the battle; you might not live to enjoy it afterwards.'

Lal turned and stared at Henry. 'It has been a battle. The battle's going on . . .'

'Oh come on, Lal, not one of your frettings.'

'We never were really suited. Henry – only at first when we used to want each other all the time. We should have parted when that cooled off. We'd had the best of each other: we'd had all the wonderful things.'

'What rubbish you do talk, Lal. As couples go, we've been among the lucky ones. You name me the day when we've had arguments. I could count them on the fingers of one hand.'

'Not arguments, Henry, but a battle going on inside . . .'

'The trouble with you, Lal, is you think too much. We're old now. God bless us, so why not give your mind a bit of a rest?'

Lal turned back to the window. 'You'll book the table, then, Henry? I do think that if we are going to Partridge's, it would be safer to book.'

*

Spring arrived on the Saturday in the shape of a deep blue sky and a softening of the breeze. Larry never opened the restaurant for lunch. 'It simply is not fair on Edwin,' he said. Instead, he usually prepared a light lunch for the two of them and they sat by themselves in the restaurant, enjoying its peace.

Edwin always washed up. He did the job so carefully that their few plates and dishes sometimes took him half an hour, a half-hour usually spent by Larry, a cigarette in his curling mouth, in blissful contemplation of his friend. He took as much care over these lunches as he did over his evening menus.

After all, he said to himself, this is our home. Edwin has a right to my time. And to cook for Edwin was pure pleasure. Often, just before sleep, his mind would turn up some little dish that he would make for Edwin as a treat the following day.

Early on the Saturday morning, wandering out onto the patio (laid in intricate patterning of stone and brick by Edwin) Larry felt the warmth of the sun and decided he would lay a table for them outside, make them a cold lunch and serve it with a bottle of hock. He imagined this meal and others like it that they would share during the coming summer, and his imaginings laid on him a hand of such pleasurable gentleness that he didn't want to move.

Indeed was poor suffering Lawrence dead! He was dead without trace and only Larry, head crammed with joy, existed now.

'Larry!'

Edwin called him from an upstairs window. Larry looked up and saw that Edwin, whom he had left sleeping, was dressed.

'I'm going out,' Edwin called.

'Where?'

'Just out.'

'Oh.'

Larry knew that he shouldn't question him. This was what Edwin hated most.

'Will you be back for lunch?' he asked.

'Yes.'

He was relieved. They would still have their lunch on the patio and now, if Edwin was going out, he could spend the whole morning in the kitchen, do some preparation for the inevitably busy Saturday evening as well.

Larry waved to Edwin, saw him nod and then disappear from the window. He made himself stay where he was till he heard Edwin's Alfa Romeo roar out of the gate. Then he wandered into the kitchen and tied on his apron.

Larry made an iced tomato and mint soup, a cold curry sauce for a roasted chicken and a watercress salad. He spread a pink cloth with matching napkins on the wooden patio table and set two careful places, each headed by a tall stemmed hock glass. He then went back into the kitchen, checked the contents of his huge fridge and larder against the evening menus for Saturday and Sunday, made a shopping list, took a basket and got into his car.

By the time I get back from shopping, he thought to himself, Edwin will be back; then I can open the hock.

*

When Lal woke on the Monday morning she experienced that bleakest of sorrows – the realisation that a dream had tricked her with a few seconds' happiness and was now gone.

She had dreamed herself young. She had dreamed a bedroom in someone's country house and a corridor outside it which creaked under Henry's footstep as in the dark he fumbled his way towards her room.

She had laughed a secretive laugh full of joy as she lay under the clean linen sheet and waited for him. Their wedding was in a few weeks' time. Then there would be no more creeping down corridors: she would be Mrs Henry Barkworth and the strong white body under the silk dressing gown that now shuffled towards her, moving slowly, prudently, but running, running like a hare in its desire for her, would lie in a big bed

78

beside her – hers. Yes, Lal remembered, there had been a great feasting of love between her and Henry. Sex had never frightened her as it seemed to frighten some women of her sheltered generation. To touch and be touched became, after Henry's rough taking of her, all. All life, save this, paled and receded into insignificance.

For days together she would not let Henry go to his office, but kept him with her in their wide, comfortable bed.

'We fit so well!' she laughed. 'How could anything be more perfect?'

Then came the War. Lal's children were both conceived during Henry's brief periods of leave and born when he was away. When the War was over and he came home, he made love to Lal like a weary stranger. She wept for what they had lost.

Lal sat up, rubbed her eyes with a white hand. It was strange that she could dream a desire she had long since ceased to feel. Life was so stale now.

'We smell bad, Henry and I,' she thought bitterly. 'We're blemished and fat and no good to anyone. Why do we go on and on?'

The day was interminable. Lal felt bilious, as if the meal they would gobble up at Partridge's was already inside her. She felt like crying. But I've shed so many tears for myself, she thought wearily, why shed more? So the evening crept towards her.

She thought as she dressed for it of the wine Henry would order: a heavy claret that they would both enjoy but which, soon afterwards, would give her indigestion and a headache. Fifty years! We've had fifty years together, so now we celebrate, but the unremarkableness of all that time, the waste of it all . . .

'Cheer up, darling.'

Henry was breezy, tugging on his braces, smelling of aftershave, his bald head gleaming.

'Oh, was I . . .?'

'You've been miles away all day, Lal. Something wrong? Not feeling up to it?'

'What? The meal?'

'No! Not just the meal – the occasion!'

'In a way not. We don't need to make any fuss, do we?'

'No, no fuss. But a bottle of fizz at least, don't you think? I asked Larry to put one on ice for us.'

'Yes.'

Lal dabbed her face with powder. She had decided to wear a black dress – the one concession to her real feelings. Pinned to the dress would be the diamond and sapphire brooch Henry had given her on their wedding day.

There was a small bar just off the dining room in Partridge's; it was too small really for all the diners who congregated there, but was pretty and restful, done up by Edwin in two shades of green. A fine tapestry drape hung down one wall and now Lal leaned back against this, her head almost touching a huntsman's knee behind her.

One of Larry's lady helpers (he had two, both about forty-five and confusingly called Myra and Moira) had brought Henry the champagne he had ordered and he was pouring it excitedly like a thirsty schoolboy might a longed-for Coke.

'This is the stuff, darling!'

Lal smiled and nodded. She often thought that the reason for Henry's pinkness of face and head was that he did simple things with such relish.

'So,' he exclaimed, holding up his own glass, 'this is it then, Lal! Happy anniversary, darling.'

Lal only nodded at Henry, then took a tiny sip of her champagne. 'It's a long time,' she said, 'since we had this.'

The restaurant was seldom full on a Monday night. The little bar was completely empty except for Henry and Lal, so that to make some accompaniment to their sipping of the champagne Lal needed to talk.

'Larry's not around, is he? He usually pops into the bar, doesn't he, with his apron on?'

'I expect he's hard at work. We wouldn't want Larry doing anything but concentrating on our dinner, would we?' Henry said jovially.

'I like Larry,' she said.

'He's a clever cook.'

'I think he's quite shy underneath all that flippety talk and showing off his bottom.'

'Lal!'

'Well, he does. Henry. He shows it off all the time. Haven't you noticed the way he ties his apron so carefully, so that the bow just bounces up and down on his behind when he walks?'

'No, I haven't noticed.'

'I mean, a less shy person wouldn't need the bow, would he?'

'Haven't a clue, Lal.'

'Oh, they wouldn't definitely. You can tell that Larry's very dependent.'

'On what?'

'Not on what – on Edward or whatever his name is: his friend. He loves that friend and depends on him. Edward's more cultured than Larry is.'

Myra (Henry addressed her as Myra; but Lal nudged him, fearing it might be Moira) came to take their order. Lal ordered Champignons à la Viennoise, followed by stuffed pork tenderloin with cherry and Madeira sauce; Henry ordered a venison terrine, followed by Veal Cordon Bleu.

Henry then chose a bottle of fine claret and sat back, one hand on his stomach, the other holding his champagne glass. It's not hard, he thought, to find ones little pleasures – just as long as one isn't poor. He smiled at Lal.

His work done for the evening, Larry took off his apron and hung it up. Only two tables had been occupied – not unusually for a Monday evening – and he hoped those few customers would leave early so that he could tidy up and go to bed. He sat down on one of his kitchen stools and took a gulp of the large whisky he had poured himself. But the whisky did nothing to lessen the pain Larry was feeling. The pain squatted there inside him, an undreamed-of but undeniable parasite.

Even his hands which usually moved so lightly and quickly were slowed by the pain, so that he had kept his few customers waiting for their meal, waiting and growing impatient. I must go out, he thought wearily, and apologise. Not do my little round to hear any praise tonight, but just go out and apologise for the delay, for the gluey quality of the Madeira sauce, for cooking the veal too long . . .

Larry sighed. He had said nothing to Myra or Moira. For three evenings he had kept going almost as if nothing had happened, so humbled and grieved by the turn his life had taken that he didn't wish to find a word, not one, to express it, but rather held it in – held it so tightly inside him that no one could suspect how changed he was, how absolutely changed.

If I can keep it in, he said to himself, then my body will assimilate it; it will become diluted and one day – perhaps? – it won't be there any more. It will have passed through me – only the vaguest memory – and gone.

'Bill for table four, Mr Partridge.' Myra, carrying four empty wine glasses, came into the kitchen.

Larry got off his stool and, taking his drink, shuffled over to the pine desk Edwin had provided for him at one end of the kitchen. He wrote out and added up the bill for a party of four – young people he had never seen before – and handed it to Myra.

If they're leaving now, Larry thought, then I don't have to go, not to the strangers. I'll wait till they've paid and gone and then I'll go and have a word with the Barkworths.

Larry liked Lal Barkworth. She looked at the world out of fierce brown eyes. Neither the eyes nor the body were still for long: only when something or someone managed to hold her elusive attention did she stop pacing and watching. Larry sensed that she tolerated him – as she seemed not to tolerate most people she met.

But remembering her staring eyes, now he felt afraid of facing her – knowing that she of all people would see at once that something had happened, that his gestures were awkward, his mind slow.

He refilled his whisky glass and sat motionless on the stool, waiting to hear the door close on the party of young people.

When he heard them leave and Myra came back into the kitchen with their money on a saucer, Larry got off the stool and, without looking in the mirror Edwin had hung above his desk to see if his hair was tidy, wandered out into the dining room.

Lal was sitting alone, smoking a cigarette. Forgetting for a moment that he had cooked two dinners, Larry wondered if she had come alone and had sat there all evening in silence. This sudden feeling of pity for her made him forget his pain just for an instant and smile at her. Lal smiled back.

Larry noticed that her brown eyes seemed bereft of some of their sharpness, almost filmed over. So it's all right then, he thought. She's drunk quite a lot; she's not seeing clearly, not into my mind – she won't guess.

'Hello, Larry dear.'

'Mrs Barkworth.' Larry held out a limp, hot hand and Lal touched it lightly.

'I expect we're keeping you up,' she said.

Larry looked round at the empty restaurant. 'Monday night – no one at the feast! Washday doesn't give one an appetite, I daresay.'

'We had a good meal.'

'Did you? Not one of my best, any of it. We all have our off nights, don't we?'

'Mine was very nice, Larry. I couldn't eat it all, I'm afraid. I never seem to be able to, not when it's something special. I used to eat well when I was young. Will you sit down Larry? Henry's gone to the loo, he won't be long.'

'Oh, yes, I see. Well . . .' Larry felt confused.

He wanted to say: "I thought you'd come alone", then realised that he'd cooked the veal for Henry Barkworth and here on the table of course were two wine glasses, two coffee cups.

He sat, gulping his whisky. Over the rim of his glass he was aware of Lal watching him.

'It isn't the same!' Larry blurted out.

There was a moment's silence; then Lal said: 'What isn't?'

'Oh . . . you know . . .' Larry couldn't finish the sentence.

To Lal's amazement, he had begun to weep, making no effort to disguise or cover his crying, his face awash with tears.

'Oh, Larry . . .'

Larry took another drink from the whisky glass, then stammered: 'I haven't told anyone. I thought I could keep it . . . inside . . . I thought no one would need to know.'

'Yes,' said Lal, quietly, 'yes.'

'But . . .' Larry put a fist up to his eyes now. 'I can't. It just isn't possible . . . when something like that . . .'

'Is it something to do with Edward?'

'Edwin. *Edwin.* That's his name. Not Edward. He was never like an Edward. Only like himself, like Edwin. And we were so happy. We were just as happy – happier – than some people married. I thought we were. I thought I knew. And I never would have left him, never in my life, so how could he . . .?'

Larry's voice was choked with his sobbing. Facing him across the table, Lal's body felt freezing cold. She reached out a hand and laid it on his arm. She was glad of the warmth of his arm under her cold hand. 'If . . .' she began.

Larry looked up. 'What?'

'If . . . he had just gone for a while perhaps, for a kind of holiday, a break from routine, well then –'

'No.'

'But why then, Larry? Why should he leave you?'

Larry pulled out a purple handkerchief and wiped his eyes. 'He . . .' Larry stopped, sucked at the whisky. 'It was on Saturday. I had thought . . . because of the sunny day, we would have lunch out on the patio. I made us the lunch. Edwin was out. I didn't know where because he didn't tell me. So I made this nice lunch for us and waited for him.

'But when he came back he said he didn't want any lunch and I said: "Edwin, I made this for you and I opened a bottle of hock and thought we could sit out in the sunshine . . ."

'He got into one of his rages. He wanted to get into a rage. He wanted me to do something silly like sulking over the meal so that he could rage at me and leave there and then. He tried to make me the excuse. He said he couldn't bear it the way I always spoiled him and did things for him and then sulked if he didn't like them, but I said: "Edwin, okay, I do that; I do that because I want you to like things and be happy with me, but that isn't enough! You couldn't leave, not for that."

'So then he had to admit – he had to admit that wasn't it. He was drunk – got himself drunk on vodkas so that he could tell me. It's someone called Dean, nineteen or something, no more than a kid. Edwin's been sleeping with him. Whenever he goes out, that's where he's gone, to sleep with him. He says he can't be . . . He says he's obsessed with him . . . He says he can't be without him.'

Larry stopped talking. His sobs were only shudders now. Lal kneaded his arm. 'Oh, Larry . . .'

'I'm sorry,' he blurted. 'I'm sorry to burden you.'

'No, Larry, I'm the one who's sorry, so sad, because I knew you had this – this precious kind of love. You see, I can't do any more for anyone now, but I was once very strong because I loved. I was so strong! I'm too old now. I just turn away. That's all I can do, isn't it, when everything's so ugly – just turn away. But you, Larry, you must fight to get him back, to get your love

back. Life is so hideous without love, Larry; it makes you want
to die.'

'Evening, Larry!'

Henry, jovially wined and full, staggered to the table.
'How's tricks, then?' he said.

*

Lal lay still. The meal lay in her stomach like a stone. Henry lay
next to her, sweating a little as he snored.

As quietly as she could, not wanting to wake Henry, Lal got
out of bed and crept to the bathroom. She made up one of her
indigestion powders and sat on the edge of the bath, watching
the powder dissolve.

When she had drunk it down, she belched and a little of the
pain left her stomach, as if the stone had been blanketed by
snow.

'There won't be another fifty, thank God,' she whispered,
staring at her empty glass; but even though she smiled at this
thought, she found that a tear had slid down her cheek on to
her lip. Lal sighed. 'Oh, well,' she whispered, 'at least for once
I'm not weeping for myself. I'm weeping for Larry.'

Current Account

'*Bronze*? I'm not as rich as I was.'

The Princesse de Villemorin crossed her still estimable legs and glared at the sunset now faded to a luminous mauve that almost matched her high-heeled sandals.

'People seem to think I'm immune from inflation. But no one is immune. Take just the servants. I'm paying them fifty per cent more than I was five years ago. So you see . . .'

The princess turned and reached out a caressing hand. Discreet turquoise bangles gently clinked as the hand came to rest on Guy's naked shoulder. The hand journeyed upwards, fingering the warm back of the neck, then tugging at the roots of hair so marvellously blond she privately compared it to the gold spun from flax in a fairytale she had long forgotten.

'Please don't be cross, darling.'

'I need the bronze, Penelope.'

'I know you do, but have you any idea what bronze in that kind of quantity costs now?'

'You can afford it.'

'Couldn't you work in lead or metal or something? You hear of terribly successful sculptors making things out of old prams these days and showing them at the Tate.'

'Not me.'

'You don't hear of anyone – except perhaps Henry Moore – working in bronze.'

'Bronze is the only substance I can relate to.'

'Substance? You make it sound like putty.'

The princess's hand tumbled as Guy rose and walked to the edge of the terrace. Beneath him, the garden lay in shadow, puffing its exotic breath at the encroaching dusk. He was aware, as he sighed, of Penelope on her chair, her body in its floating dress, her eyes watching, possessing, her thought: *without my money he can't work*. Anger welled up, familiar yet absurd. *One day, I will leave her.*

'Of course,' came her silky voice, 'you can have the bronze. Guy? Listen to me, darling. You can have the bronze. I'll ring my stockbroker in the morning and arrange the money. It's only that sometimes . . .'

'What?'

'I wish you'd be more grateful.'

Guy was silent, smelling the white flowers shaped like stars that climbed the terrace wall. His mind charged to her morning ceremonial, she exquisitely in place on her satin sheets, her body massaged and tremulous with its invitation, her eyes lidded with silver, sparkler-fizzing for the first touch of him. And the weight she demanded, the strength that had to clutch and devour so that her face lay buried in his neck, his dragon-panting fanning her hair, his sweat sucking his belly to hers, her deep and buried sigh of triumph as she used him up.

I wish you'd be more grateful.

*

She is fifty-five. She is twenty-three years older than me. She could have borne me.

The thought followed Guy from her bed to his studio. On entering the high room, he'd perch on a stool and will the thought to settle in the plaster dust, become obliterated in his work. Because here – only here – was he safe from her. This was Bluebeard's room, the one the Princesse de Villemorin couldn't enter. Once it had been a laundry. Far into the twentieth century, women had slapped and pummelled the soiled linen of the châtelaine on stones worn to glimmering. Now it held the quiet of his inspiration. Nothing moved in it but Guy and the straining forms imprisoned first in clay, then finally in bronze.

As the sculptor worked, he chose to forget, if he could, the presence of the Princesse de Villemorin embarked upon the journey of each sumptuous day, little chiselled heels clacking over sunlight on her polished floors, voice dealing faultless instructions to the sallow-faced people she called *les domestiques*, pointed fingers rearranging a bowl of roses, fluttering from the roses to the rosewood bureau to gather the telephone, to pick up a gold pen and begin to notate in ruled columns, ankles crossed now, the body at peace with its arithmetic. *I wish you'd be more grateful . . .*

She disturbs me. In every sense of this word, she is a disturbing woman. If she was French, she would disturb me less; it's the Englishness staring out of her French name – the Princesse Penelope de Villemorin – that gives her away to me and makes me loathe where (I have vowed to my art) I must try to love. Yet she says she belongs to France now. When she snoozes in the afternoons, she has nightmares of the old prince her husband and the line of noble cousins, nephews (yet not children) dangling from his limbs to weigh him down with magisterial expectations and with a voice bleeting sorrow for the gravest of his failures, his bitter marriage. Mon dieu, mon dieu, an English divorcee and a Protestant, snickered the ancient trussed-up de Villemorin aunts. What a blow for the *famille*! What a muddying of the line! 'I was married to him for eight years,' said Penelope, 'and that family taught me nothing except how to hate them.'

Oh but they taught you how to value money! That was the legacy of the marriage, the one you used against them after the prince left you. Poor old prince, with his exquisite nails. He wanted to tear your flesh with his nails for squandering all that he gave you, for wasting it all, wasting his love. Yet he put on a clean silk shirt, tied his paisley tie from Simpson's of Piccadilly, clicked his heels at eight years of marriage and walked out without touching you or seeing you again. And you squawked like a macaw for the best lawyers. You scented a fortune and it hung like a whiff of tar in solicitors' rooms, crouched just out of sight in the creases of solicitors' smiles. You knew you should get half. But the family fought you. All with their filbert nails and perfected manners, they fought you like cockerels. So you settled for a lump sum. You stopped sniffing the tar smell of 'half'. The lump sum was more than enough.

Or so you thought then, when it was you alone, Penelope – no longer a princess, but still calling yourself one – and moved in alone to your pretty château 'with it's own historical laundry and stabling for five cars'. But the years picked at it. Your own tastes became richer: the aloneness of you sought compensation. And the menopausal Penelope mourned the dying out of beauty. You touched the crevices of your body and remembered the gaudy kisses of the young. One night, you started going to the town in your Mercedes, drinking a crème de menthe in one of the bars and driving home with a young man's head in your lap. For a while, the young men were cheap. And then, in the same bar, in the same way, I met you.

*

The butler, Maurice, announced dinner.

Penelope adjusted the thin heelstrap of a mauve shoe and stood up. 'Come on, Guy darling. Stop pouting and put your shirt on. I've told you, we'll arrange for the shipment of bronze. I was only teasing about the old prams.'

She held out her arm, waiting for his hand to steer her inside to the candlelit dining room, but he was fussing with his shirt, his face turned away from her.

'Hurry up, darling. I want to talk to you over dinner, about Lorna.'

'What about Lorna?'

'I've got a letter from her, full of all her dull goings on in Australia. But it seems she's coming to Europe and wants to see me.'

'Why does she want to see you?'

'Money, I suppose. Why else do stubborn daughters creep back to mothers they affect to despise? But God knows, on a teacher's salary, how she can afford the airfare.'

Guy tucked his shirt inside the pale blue trousers the princess had bought for him in Paris. There were moments, and this was one of them, when Penelope de Villemorin felt impaled by her own yearnings. *Sainte Marie, let him never leave me.*

'Come along, Guy. Anita has made a soufflé and it will spoil.'

So they sat close to each other in the pretty dining room and were served. Guy noticed, in between forkfuls of the soufflé, that Penelope had begun to economise on her wines: the Pouilly-Montrachet he had learned to expect had been replaced by a cheap local Loire wine. He longed to ask her suddenly precisely how rich she was. Tell me *precisely*, he wanted to say, how much money and what assets you own. But certain questions breed for a lifetime and are never uttered. He would ask her instead about the gallery.

'The gallery?'

'Yes.' Guy wondered why she sounded surprised.

'Well, what can I tell you? You know it all already. Our policy is sound in my view. We search for young painters and help them on their way. We create fashions.'

'And your stake was half?' The word never lost its particular meaning for the princess.

'I believe it's an excellent investment – and a lovely excuse to go to Paris more often! Of course, one could wish that returns were higher. It seems not enough collectors are prepared to take the financial risks on new artists.'

'Art isn't a commodity, Penelope.'

'Oh no! I didn't mean to imply that. But as you yourself know, it's a very costly business. Art would simply not exist without the rich.'

'Of course it would exist!'

'Well exist, yes, but no one could live by it. Anyway darling, let's not argue. There's no earthly reason we couldn't give you an autumn show at the gallery.'

'And you take sixty per cent of everything I sell!'

Penelope smiled. She noticed, fleetingly, that the prawns in the soufflé echoed perfectly the colour of the dining-room walls.

'I expect,' she said, 'we could make an exception in your case.'

*

The princess couldn't sleep. She went to the rosewood bureau. She re-read Lorna's letter, written in large writing she had always considered plain and lacking in character. The letter told her that Lorna (now twenty-eight by Penelope's calculations) would 'take advantage, this year, of a European summer vacation'. The visit to the château was planned for August.

Memories of her daughter ('always clever, Penelope. Lorna was always clever . . .') made her fidget with guilt and irritation. She tugged at a piece of stiff writing paper and began: 'My dear Lorna, I'm so very sorry to say that an August visit won't be possible as I shall be travelling . . .' but quickly crumpled it. The clever girl would find some way to see her. The clever girl's eyes would ferret among the telltale creases of fifty-five years and decide with satisfaction, Mother's power is waning. Oh it was cruel, miserable! Why ever had this teacher daughter decided to poke and pry after eight blissful years of separation and silence?

She pulled out her portfolio (how it had dwindled!) of stocks and shares. How utterly miserable to be selling off yet more. But the bronze, though. She must find a way to purchase this wretched bronze for Guy. The princess rubbed her eyes, puffy from snatched sleep. *Money is power.* So whispered the de Villemorin aunts, clucking over each her own fortune. They died in their bonnets and were buried unmourned. The money was shared among the cousins who squandered it, so complained the prince, on American luxuries, not forgetting American women . . .

The sun came up beyond the steep apple orchards. The house began to murmur with the tiptoeing of servants. It was the hour when the princess usually rose and washed her body, before presenting it, creamed and scented, to Guy. *Obliterate me*, said this scented yearning body. But this morning, immobile at her desk, the princess felt too tired.

*

The bronze and Lorna arrived the same day, 10 August. Guy stood in the laundry, fingering the blackish lumps, beautiful as yet only by their incredible weight.

A stubbornly hot fortnight and the death of the one stockbroker she trusted had ravaged the poise of the princess. She had enraged Guy by drinking more wine than she could hold and wailing in her little-girl's voice that she had never been loved. As he touched the bronze, the sun falling on his wide hand, he tried not to measure the price he was paying for this precious metal.

He stayed in the laundry studio all day, working in clay. When the sun dipped from the high windows, he came out into the hot evening. He was tired. He longed to lie down in a cool bed, alone.

He showered and changed (this much I can do for Penelope's daughter) and went to find the two women. Penelope looked glittering. As a defence against Lorna's arrival, she had had her hair re-tinted, she had draped her body in a white, off-the-shoulder dress. She fingered the pearl choker clenched at her neck. 'This is Lorna. Lorna, this is Guy who . . . has the old laundry house as his studio. He's a very, very talented sculptor, aren't you darling?'

Lorna got up. The flamboyant introduction had seemed to demand movement of some kind. Guy saw a thin, bony girl with clever brown eyes and thick hair cut very short. She wore an Indian dress, skimpy and creased. Her breasts, covered by this whisper of material, seemed oddly plump, the only part of her body that betrayed any blood tie with her mother. Her smile suggested a knowingness that must surely irritate Penelope.

'My mother didn't say you were here.'

Australia. Yes, he could see it now, the woman-stayed-girl at twenty-eight. Freckled. Nourished by enormous skies.

Guy held out his hand, tried to stare past the smile.

'You've come a long way.'

'Yes. But then it's years since I saw Mother. I expect she told you.'

'Lorna loves the house, Guy.'

Penelope had never attempted to quell the enjoyment she got from showing other people her riches. Why bother with Aubusson carpets if no one ever admires them? And Lorna had clearly been astonished by the château and its treasures. She had remembered her mother was rich, yet seemed to have forgotten that riches can gleam at you from surfaces you can touch and smell.

'And she's going to stay for ten days, which is wonderful for me. So much to catch up on, haven't we Lorna?'

Oh yes, thought the Australian girl. But surely you understand that that's precisely why I came over, to get a full account of a life I've only allowed myself to guess at since you left my father and married the stiff and straight prince and became wealthy. And of course you never told me about the sculptor, young enough to be my brother. You left me to imagine you getting old by yourself. I thought at last time had punished you.

Guy sat down. Penelope reached for the champagne in its brimming bucket and poured him a glass. The sun on the terrace was still warm. He took the glass from Penelope and turned to the daughter. Her eyes were lowered, seeming to contemplate her slim, dusty feet in flat sandals.

'To Lorna!' said Guy.

*

The nights are extraordinary, thought Lorna. So perfectly peaceful. Mother has created an 'island'. In it, everything breathes as ordained by her, and the world outside, the world I know of cramped rooms and pushing your body into the little corner of sun left on your balcony after four o'clock in the blistering Sydney summers, exists beyond. Useless to tell her of that other world. In it, for her, exists only terror, and she doesn't want to look. Sufficient that the stockbroker died. That was terror enough! She still talks of it: 'With my kind of money, you have to be careful, you see Lorna. Because people can milk you. I'm being milked by everyone. By the servants, by accountants and even by the gallery in Paris. I honestly don't believe I'm getting my due on my investment. And this spring, I was forced to sell the one mingy tiara given to me by belle-mère de Villemorin. Luckily I know Arnaud Clerc of the Bijouterie Clerc in Paris, or even that could have gone for next to nothing . . .'

Oh Mother, what deafening complaint clanks across the acres of quiet, so carefully tended! I can hear your mind stoking its engines of dissatisfaction, even as you sit on your terrace, so poised, reaching for the bottle in the ice bucket, reaching for the sculptor's smile. Fears group and regroup in you. Your white dress, at dinner, was splashed with some reddish sauce or other. You looked to the sculptor for help, but he turned away. He turned to me with his smile, yet all I could do was stare. Because what does an artist do to himself if he locks himself inside Mother's island? What are you doing? Working you say, but working in an old laundry where women were paid a pittance to plunge their red arms into the stained, suddy water of the unassailably rich. How has Mother stained you? Guy, the sculptor. Why do you smile at me when, even this minute perhaps, Mother opens her arms and receives you like a gift of amber, spreads you on her like an ointment – your youth to heal her age.

Yet there is something. Not in you, Guy, as much as in me. Some feeling that made me turn away, made me gabble about myself, telling jokes about my Head of Department to see if you laughed and showing off my clever self ('Lorna is so unlike you, Penelope dear,' said long-ago friends) to let you know there was substance inside the shorn head, inside the cheap Indian dress so marvellously wrong for Mother's dining room.

And you listened. You watched. Mother buys you. She buys you afresh each day. But a look in you – and in me – lets me believe I could have you free.

*

'Promise me,' whispered Penelope, 'that you won't.'

Half asleep, deliciously comfortable in the enfolding satin, Guy mumbled ambiguous assent, let the princess caress the side of his face, then slipped with perfect ease into a dream of Lorna. He was bathing in a river. Lorna waded in from a rock, still wearing the skinny dress which, once wetted, clung to her. He gazed at her eyes, lashes flecked with water like minuscule diamonds. When he kissed her, her tongue was long and gentle.

The princess wanted to pull him back from sleep. It was as if, sleeping, Guy deserted her. She said his name. He lay still and golden beside her, barely covered. Look at him, she wanted to wail to the ghost of the prince walled up in some mausoleum near Tours, look at my lover!

*

The princess had never known such terrible days. Ten in all, she reminded herself. After ten days, she will be gone. She belongs in the history classroom. She belongs in some ugly suburb. Only Guy and I belong here, with my treasures that keep us safe, with each our own role to play.

'I hate having my role confused, darling.'

'Your role?'

'Yes. Lorna confuses my role, Guy.'

The laugh was mocking, ungentle. The princess looked up sharply. 'Guy, you did promise me, didn't you?'

'Promise you?'

'That you wouldn't. You wouldn't ever, would you?'

'I already have.'

Not merely in his dreams. He and Lorna had gone walking early on the fourth morning of the ten. The princess sat in bed with her silver breakfast tray, calling Paris, calling London, too preoccupied with the telephone to imagine they could be gone all morning, gone still at lunchtime, eating joyously in a little café with memories of their morning bright in their eyes. Yet what made him admit it? What made him decide not to lie, when lying was so easy? *You believe what you want to believe.*

'Oh Guy . . .' Penelope's hands were rammed against her mouth. Guy stared, horrified. For a second, he imagined that neither words nor tears would come gushing out from between the fingers, but blood.

'Penelope . . .'

'Don't speak! I can't listen to anything!'

'It was terribly innocent, Penelope.'

'Innocent! Don't Guy! *Don't*! You make me want to be sick. You make me want to die!'

The act innocent because so joyful, he thought, yet the inspiration cruel: two people who approach each other, aware of the invisible onlooker, whose torment drives them on. As they enfold each other, there she is in the touch and push of their bodies, there she is tangled in their moist hair, there she is in their breaths. And afterwards – the glorious knowledge that together they had conquered her, where each had failed to conquer alone. As they walk back, they hear it, the click-clack of Penelope's high heels, the clink and trinkle of Mother's bracelets. Perfect, thinks Guy. Perfect, thinks Lorna.

*

The Princesse de Villemorin sat alone by the first fire of September. The London accountant had been and gone, the Paris gallery owner had been and gone. She was left with their sums and her misery.

Maurice announced himself. Penelope sipped at her whisky and didn't turn. A reminder, Madame, says Maurice, only a *reminder* that no one in the château has received any *salaire* this month . . .

She waved him away. Let them all desert her. Nothing mattered any more. Only the plans she made in the golden whisky haze: she would buy bronze in quantities no mortal could dream of owning, she would fill the laundry with bronze, she would lay her head on the vast, unmoving lumps of bronze and let her tears flow onto its darkness.

I know him, she whispers to the spent fire, I know he will trade his Sydney teacher (firm though her breasts are, clever though her damned head has always been) for his own statues. The artist in him will win and without money the artist in him will pine. The mouldering de Villemorin jewels will go. They must all go. And Maurice must realise that no one can be paid now, not till I have wedged that studio with what he calls his 'substance'. Life drowns and gurgles in the sea of the whisky glass. Life sleeps. I am Sleeping Beauty ('What a joke, at your age, Mother!') and I refuse to wake up till the prince has picked his way through the briars and grown roses of my daughter's mind and comes crashing down here, his weight as potent as the weight of bronze, to crush me and still me with life.

Guy stayed with Lorna till his money and the summer ran out, then made his way south to the Princesse de Villemorin's château.

On her long flight home to Sydney, Lorna ate none of the food offered her and stayed absolutely still in her seat, talking to no one. Around her parting from Guy, a man who, had she found him before he strayed into a bar one night and met her mother, she believed she might have loved, she concocted an essay subject for her sixth-form students: "What is the function of the creative artist in our materialistic society?" She saw the blackboard where she would write up the title. She saw the thirty or so faces staring at it with anxious frowns. One of the girls raised her hand. 'Please, miss, I don't understand.'

Words With Marigold

I don't know why me. I don't know why you want to talk to me. I'm no different from anyone. I mean, there are hundreds – thousands – of girls like me, aren't there? Perhaps you're going to talk to us all, are you? Lost Generation, or whatever it is they call us. I've always wondered how they do surveys. I bet they take a tiny sample of people and call it a silent majority. I mean, I bet they can't be bothered to go round asking hundreds of people the same stupid questions. Except I met one on a train once. A survey person. She tried to make me answer things like 'How frequently do you travel on this train?' I said, that's my business, *dearie,* I said I don't own much, but I own what I do and why I do it. She went puce. I followed her down into First Class and she got this group of men in business suits and they invited her to sit down. I suppose it was a great day for them. I suppose they'd been longing for years for someone to ask them what they were doing on that train! They were drinking whiskies an' that. They travelled on that train every day.

I'm not extraordinary though. I suppose it's considered extraordinary to have a termination at sixteen, but I can tell you it isn't, if that's what you're thinking. I mean, it's no more extraordinary than having a fuck. In fact, that's all it is, if you think about it. A screw. With consequences. No one worries about anyone having a screw, less they're real actual kids or something. But try getting a termination at sixteen. I mean the stuff you have to put up with. Fine till they suss your age. I mean, perfectly okay an' that, but then they start on at you. They start implying your whole life could be fucked, like you've screwed your whole personality and your whole chances and you're psychologically damaged. They want to make you start believing these things or they wouldn't just act like that, would they? And the stuff about your parents. They imply your Mum's to blame or something because you're too young to think for yourself. They say things like, 'Was your Mother aware of your relationship?' So I said, no love, my Mum's not aware of any sodding thing these days. She's out of her mind most of the time on Special Brew. And her eyes are going as well – disappearing inside her flesh. She's put on three stone since last year.

But actually that is when things started to get bad. I'd have said I was quite alright, like you know, quite happy till that all began. I was working for my O-levels. Biology was my best subject. Biology and Art, but they said you can't take Art. I was okay at Maths. Not fantastic, you know, but okay. I could have got something like a C or something. Eddie used to help me with Maths. I mean quite a lot. Not just five minutes to get you through your homework, but he'd sit down with me when Mum was getting tea and he used to say, Marigold, you've got this tendency to think in straight lines and what I've got to do is to help you think in circles or spirals. He had a name for this kind of thinking. He was very interesting about it and it really started to help me because I'd tended to think there was always one way of doing something and this was the *meant* way. Because at school they never noticed things like how you were thinking, I mean they didn't have time, did they, but Eddie said he'd make time and he did.

I really enjoyed Maths homework after Eddie started to help me. I'd bring extra work home and you could just hear the teachers thinking God, Marigold Rickards taking extra Maths to do at home! But my results got better. It was terrific seeing the results get good. I mean, let's not exaggerate. I'd never be a mathematician or anything, like I could be a painter probably if I could get into art school and get my technique better. I still think I could be a painter. I mean I haven't lost hope, have I, and I know about one of the medical aspects of people in depressions is they lose hope. They just look into the future and see black or brown or something, just some dark colour and nothing in it. But I don't. I mean, I even write letters to people asking them for money to help me get through art college. I don't get any money back, but I keep writing, don't I, so that must be a good sign. I wrote to Lady Falkender. Someone told me she was a patron of the arts or whatever. Do you think she'll write back or send me something? I mean, I don't know. I can't really imagine how Lady Falkender lives, can you? I don't know if she'd write to someone like me.

I've thought of writing to Eddie, except neither of us – my Mum nor me – know his address. And I bet it wouldn't do any good to write. But it did all start then, when I think about it. Till Eddie left our house I think we were alright. They'd have rows, Eddie and my Mum, but not terrible ones. He never hit her. I mean, don't get me wrong, he wasn't at all a violent person. He liked jokes. He'd make jokes the minute he woke up. Sometimes his jokes got on my wick, but other times I'd think, he kind of keeps us all going and if he weren't here or something we'd probably have nothing to laugh at and we'd just go quiet like I suppose we must have been before. I suppose when I think about it, I dreaded the idea of Eddie leaving us. I mean I knew my Mum would just go to bits, because you could tell what he was to her. There was nothing she wouldn't do for him. He got the works. Best food she could afford, terrific ironing, thermos washed up, cufflinks and stuff at Christmas . . .

It was the age difference, I think. They were about the same age about, but she looked older. I don't blame him. He was with us for seven years and that's quite long, isn't it? I mean, I was nine or nearly nine when he came. And he never said, I don't think he said Marigold's a fucking nuisance and got me palmed off with neighbours. He just accepted me and treated me like his own kid. I mean, better than some fathers are to their kids. Quite a bit better. Like helping me with my Maths I told you about. And other things. They used to go on outings to London and he'd always say, let's take Marigold, she should have the chance to see the big city an' that. His favourite thing in London was the Science Museum. He knew masses about some of the old compasses and chronometers. There was this man who invented a type of chronometer and he was a kind of hero for Eddie. Harrison. I don't know which century he was. Before Nelson, probably.

My Mum wasn't too interested in chronometers, actually. But I don't think it was that. I mean, you wouldn't leave someone because they weren't interested in something, would you? I think it was definitely the other girl he met. She was some sort of secretary at the engineering works where he worked. I only saw her once, but I think she was quite kind of posh an' spoke all terrific an' wore skirts with linings in them. Know the type I mean? She wasn't specially pretty or anything. Not that I could see. But she was lots younger than my Mum. I'd say she was twenty-eight or nine. And I think she hypno-tised Eddie by being this different kind of person and he'd come home and start correcting my Mum's grammar. And my Mum got scared. I mean, this was the pitiful thing. She got frightened she'd say things wrong. She *wanted* her grammar to be better, to please Eddie. And food. He bought my Mum a book called French Cooking Explained. She tried to do things from it for a bit till she sussed the flippin' insult in all that. Then she put the book in the oven and the oven caught fire and that was the first time I ever saw Eddie really angry with her. I heard him yelling at her and I came down and the kitchen was covered with white stuff from the fire extinguisher, and then my Mum rushed past me and up to the toilet and sicked up. I think she knew that was the end with Eddie. I don't think she'd heard about the girl at work by then. But she knew it was all over for her. I mean, you do, I think. Don't you think? One minute you don't know and then another one minute passes and that's the crucial one, like going into a ghost train, know what I mean? Like this one minute is much longer than even longer, darker things like ghost trains. D'you get it? I got it there and then. I could see that was the crucial minute and our lives wouldn't go on like they were.

My Mum blames Eddie. She thinks she's finished now. She's only forty-four. Eddie left some socks and things behind and she burned these in the yard. I started going off her when she did this. Up till then, I'd felt really sorry for her. I'd hear her crying through the wall. I used to make a tray of tea and go and sit on her bed. Waste of time though. She'd just snivel about 'getting even' and I went off her when she'd start on this. 'Cos it's Eddie's life as well as hers, isn't it? Like in my case it's Alan's life as well as mine. Least, that's what I've had to tell myself. No one's got control. You can be a king of somewhere or the head of a billion-pound corporation or whatever and still get clobbered. Only thing is you've got money if you're a king or something or the head of a billion-pound whatsit. So you can go to art college. Providing they'll take you. You don't have to write begging letters to people. And you've got O-levels.

My Maths got terrible. I'd relied on Eddie, hadn't I? I couldn't get myself to think in spirals or whatever. I lost the knack. So I knew I wouldn't get Maths O. Not even a C or something. I could have got biology because my drawings were good, I mean they looked professional and the drawings are half of it with biology: cross-section of the broad bean, mucor heads, habitat of the brown water beetle ... I don't know about Eng Lit. I might have got it. *As You Like It* we did. Alan told me *As You Like It* is quite an important play, but I kept thinking, I don't know what they're doing exactly.

I think I'm attracted to people who want to help me. Or they're attracted to me. Alan wanted to help me. I went to get my Mum out of the pub one night, 'cos she couldn't move. She was sitting in a corner, sweating. She used to dribble when she got to this state. Dribble and burp and sometimes sick up. Now I can't stand to see a person drunk. Specially her. I run a mile. I can't go near them or touch them. Alan helped me out with her. I got her to bed and Alan stayed. I don't mean he forced himself on me. I mean, what I did was talk. Like I'm talking to you, but better, because I was deeply attracted to Alan. I mean I'd had some boys, Badger Reid from school and Billy Tansley who thought he was Don Juan 'cos he'd got a second-hand Suzuki! But they were for laughs. Rubbish! Alan was older, see. I mean he was a mature man.

He had this cottage. It's called Green End. It's down a track, miles from anything. He thinks the world of it. He says if he lived in town, he'd wind up killing someone. I don't think he likes people. He likes women. He's a very attractive man.

He didn't seduce me or anything. It was five or something in the morning when I shut up talking and he just lay me down where we were in front of the fire in the front room. I was wearing my school skirt and he came all over it so as not to come inside me. He said coming on my skirt was the most exciting sexual experience he'd ever had. Men say these things, don't they? They say things to make you feel special. I mean, I know that now, but I didn't exactly know it then. So I've learned something haven't I? Means it wasn't all just a waste.

Alan had this handmade kiln in his garden. He'd built it himself, brick by brick. It was fate he was in the pub that one night, because he didn't go out hardly ever. He stayed at Green End and did his pottery. He let me make a pot once, but it was rubbish. He had a university degree from Oxbridge. I knew Oxbridge was two places by the time I met Alan, but I used to think they were one place. I don't think my Mum even knows what Oxbridge is! If you said, what's Oxbridge, Mum? she'd say something like stock cubes. Eddie once told me she was ignorant. Eddie said it was sad when young people got older not knowing anything. He tried to make me promise I'd go on to A-levels and get to university if I could. He said qualifications were everything these days.

My Mum got ill that night after Alan came. I had to stay home from school and try to stop her drinking, the doctor said. What a laugh, eh? I had to stop her going out to buy beer. Fat chance. She was down the off-licence soon as she could stand up, then down the pub. She looked like death. Like a suet roly-poly. She wasn't cared, though, was she? An' she never give me a thought, what I'd done for her. I mean, the day Eddie left, she lost interest in me.

Billy Tansley gave me a lift on his bike to Alan's place. Charged me a quid for the ride, greedy little bugger. Nothing's for nothing, he said. Wanted to charge me another quid for promising not to tell where I was, but I wasn't playing. You tell the whole effing street, if you want to, Billy, I said.

Alan got really excited when he saw me arrive. I mean, to have me coming to him and asking him to help me just gave him a gigantic hard-on. I'd put my uniform on again and I'd washed and ironed the skirt and he just grabbed me by the shoulders the minute he saw me and took me into his kitchen and fucked me against his fridge. You could hear bottles or something falling over inside the fridge 'cos we jogged it so hard. And I thought, God, this guy's the most fantastic person. I mean passionate. I mean, I got him really hyped up, you know, like a desperate animal.

He loved cooking, Alan. He made this terrific vegetarian thing for me the first evening I was there. He said I had beautiful breasts. He wanted me to eat his meal with my tits showing. He told me he had dreams of girls like me when he was married. He said they got in the way of normal marital relations. He said actually these dreams had destroyed his marriage.

His bed was really good, not like normal beds. He had Indian hangings on it and the sheets smelled like he'd been waving josticks over them. I really liked that bed. The nights I spent in it were the best of my life. I used to come all the time. I mean, he knew what to do. He'd been married. He wasn't like Billy Tansley or Badger Reid, those babies. And he came masses. After the first times, he didn't bother getting out when he came. He said to come inside me was the realisation of ten years of dreaming.

I don't know why I go on about him, I mean how wonderful he was and everything. I don't know why I'm telling you all these private sexual things. I mean, I should have forgotten him, that's what everyone says. I shouldn't keep letting myself remember. But it's not exactly remembering. I mean, all those things I had with Alan are just *there*, they're still in me if you know what I mean? I still wake up and think, it can't have happened, what did happen. I still sometimes think I'm in that bed and then we'll have this day in front of us, the kind of day when Alan works at his pottery and I'm just there adoring him, like I was his wife or something . . .

It was a long way to school from Green End. I used to bike it on Alan's bike when I felt like it. But I'd gone right off work and off the other girls. I mean, they used to say crap like 'Billy Tansley told us you got a sugar-daddy, Marigold.' And you should have seen the rubbish they were going with! Those schoolboys couldn't make anyone feel like a woman. They couldn't make a *woman* feel like a woman! They were wankers. Didn't know a thing about passion. So I felt superior. Who wouldn't? Only thing I got better at at school was Eng Lit. Alan knew masses about Shakespeare. He knew what everything meant. He explained *As You Like It* to me from beginning to end. No, I got bloody cheesed off with school, though. Bossy teachers. Girls boasting about their spotty blokes. I was ready to give it up, except Alan kept saying just what Eddie had said – got to stick it out at school till you get the exams. And I think they were right. I regret it now that I had to pack it in.

My Mum turned up one day. She looked a bit better, but she wasn't. She's on the booze now an' that's it. I thought, go on,

Ma, do the mother bit. Tell your daughter she's filth. Tell her she's sweet sixteen and chucking her life away on a man of thirty-eight. I was wrong, though. She'd just come for a look. Alan made her a cup of tea and I could tell she was watching her grammar. He impressed her alright. She'd never met anyone like him. I think maybe she even fancied him, 'cos she started on about herself, telling him what a beauty she'd been before she got fat. But she disgusted him. He'd seen her that night in the pub. He thought she was awful, the pits. He pushed her out after we'd had the tea and she looked really hurt like as if she wanted to be invited to stay.

I never thought I'd wind up back with her. You bloody learn though, don't you? You think you've got something made. I did. I mean, I had in a way. If I'd been older and known more about everything and if I'd layed off a bit and not been the kind of slave I was to Alan, then he might have, well, you know, fallen in love with me. I don't say he would. I mean, when I think about it, I realise I'm not clever enough for a man like that, and they want more than sex after a while, they want you to know things and recognise famous paintings and understand Shakespeare and decide how you're going to vote and things like that. He liked my drawings, though. He said I could be a good artist if I got a better understanding of why I drew things the way I do. I never thought that aspect was important in drawing, but perhaps it is. If I went to art school, they'd help me with this, wouldn't they? I dunno. Don't suppose I'll ever get there, anyway. You've got to have A-level for art school, haven't you? It's not just a question of the money.

I thought of telling Lady Falkender about the baby. I think I need to talk to someone in a letter or something because quite often I feel clobbered by all that and I start to go down like I am now and not wash or eat or take care of myself. I don't cry. I just think about it and then I get this drained feeling, like being numb and losing touch with gravity or something. I hardly told anyone at the time. I mean, I told Alan because I told him I don't mind having it if it's yours and mine, in fact I'd love to have a little baby and care for it. But he didn't want it. He didn't even want to hear about it and he gave me this long lecture about his wife who spent nine years trying to have a baby and how she came almost to full term twice and then had miscarriages and how she suffered. It was like he hated me for wanting the baby his wife had wanted. He'd gone off me a bit after my Mum came, but now he went off me really. I'd hang around him, hoping we could make love and he'd be like he'd been at the beginning, all hot an' that. I'd put my uniform on and go and kiss him on the mouth and push myself against him. Sometimes we'd fuck, but he didn't kiss me or hold me afterwards. He'd fuck with his eyes shut, like he'd get turned off if he looked at me.

He arranged everything. He got me an appointment with some Pregnancy Advice Group. He said, don't worry, Marigold, I'll see you through the actual abortion. But it was finished by then. He despised me. He thought I was stupid to have got pregnant. He said it was the fault of my upbringing. He said the working classes were still miles behind, specially the women, just stupid and ignorant.

His wife's back with him now. I biked out to see him just the one time when the thing was over, the termination I mean. I suppose I thought, if I can't have his baby, perhaps I can still have him. I don't know what made me think this. You're naive at sixteen, I guess. You hope for things you'll never get, I mean probably never get in your whole lifetime. But I thought, I've done what he wanted, got rid of the baby, so he owes me something. But there was this woman there. Someone about his age or a bit younger. She was ever so slim and she walked like she'd once been a dancer. I hadn't a clue who she was. She just came out and stared at me and said, 'I'm Alan's wife. What do you want?' I could have told her, couldn't I? I mean I could have just given it to her, the nights I'd been there and the baby and those dreams of schoolgirls he'd confessed. I could have let her have it all. But it wouldn't have changed anything. It was like when Eddie left our home. You couldn't have made him change his mind.

And I know I've got to get on now. Look at me. I look terrible, don't I? My Mum says there's a job going at the turkey place where she works an' I ought to try to get it. I hate turkeys and meat of any kind. It's probably gone by now, anyway, the job. And I get depressed about not getting my O-levels. I mean, there was a time when I could have got Maths even, and I can imagine Eddie being ever so pleased and taking us out for a celebration at the Wimpey. I don't feel rancour, though. I mean, like I said, it's Eddie's life, isn't it, and Alan's life and you've got to make the best of what's left. Otherwise you just go down. And I don't want to go down, but I wish Lady Falkender would write to me. I mean, I've got hopes of that 'cos I think she's the kind of person who might understand. I could be wrong though. I've been wrong about a lot of things.

Autumn in Florida

'Special security passes,' said the travel agent to George, 'are needed for anyone staying at Palmetto Village. I shall require a passport-sized photograph of both you and your wife. These will be forwarded to Palmetto, together with your reservation documents, photostats of the first five pages of your passports – to include, of course, your US visa – and a signed statement by a professional person – doctor, solicitor or JP, say, – vouching both for the likeness of the photographs and for your suitability as a Palmetto resident.'

It was July in Ipswich and stifling in the travel agent's stuffy premises. George loosened his tie and prepared to comment that this seemed like a lot of unnecessary fuss and paraphernalia and red tape and smacked, furthermore, of the CIA, but sighed instead and nodded and thought, the central purpose of this holiday is recovery – recovery from mediocrity, recovery from my everyday self – so I must make absolutely certain that all the arrangements go smoothly and that nothing upsets me. 'Fine,' he snapped.

While the travel agent's fingers began a repetitive waltz with his Compu-108, George picked up the Palmetto brochure. He'd owned an identical one since January and knew the pictures in it by heart: palm-fringed pale and empty beach, palm-fringed yachts jostling for space at a clean and sparkling marina, palm-fringed 18-hole golf course, 'exclusive to Palmetto residents', palm-fringed riverside nightclub hung with orange mandarin lamps, palm-fringed Palmetto Village itself, clusters of pale pink Mexican-style apartments, white umbrellas on rooves and balconies, oleander and hibiscus and Cana lilies framing the buildings not only with bright pink and orange, but also, in George's mind, with certainty. This was no mock-up, no deception: this was the tropical land limb where presidents sipped at brief idleness. While the driving October rains brought down the oak leaves and flooded the Suffolk ditches, here would George be, renewing himself.

*

George's wife, Beryl, had said at Christmas, it's been a bad year. What you mean, offered George, is you haven't got used to Jennifer being married and not here any more. No, said Beryl, I haven't, but it's not only that.

George understood. He sat in his office at the Wakelin All Saints branch of the Mercantile and General Bank, sipped the weak coffee he had taught his secretary to make and decided, Beryl knows I've been passed over. There's no fooling Beryl. She's heard me murmur about the managership and even though I haven't told her they'll bring a younger man in, she knows they will, a younger man from Head Office probably, cutting his razor-sharp teeth on the Wakelin All Saints branch.

The Wakelin All Saints branch of the Mercantile and General Bank occupied a low, Tudor building that had once been two workers' cottages. Rescued from years of decay in the sixties by a hairdresser called Maurice, they had given brief but unlikely houseroom to backwash basins, driers, mirror tables, infra-red lamps and black imitation leather chairs. But Wakelin All Saints was, as Maurice was forced eventually to point out, 'a far cry from Upper Brook Street'. His dream of combining his hairdressing skill with his yearning for silence and home-grown mange-tout peas collapsed in 1971 and Mercantile and General snapped up his premises. Maurice moved to Billericay, George was installed at Wakelin All Saints as assistant manager. Maurice was thirty-five and a sadder man; George was then forty-nine and optimistic.

Optimism was an essential ingredient of George's nature. Without it, he believed he might have suffered, particularly as he aged, the kind of despair that had driven his mother to hurl herself out of a flying fairground car at Clacton to a grossly foreseen death on a knitting of steel girders. He hadn't seen her die, but his imagination supplied every terrible detail of the body's fall, its breaking and bursting. Though forever afterwards afraid of heights, George knew that he was more afraid of the mind's plummet to darkness, fearing that here was a phenomenon that might overcome him as easily, as seductively as his occasional cravings for young women. Sometimes, he imagined it in the form of a tornado hurling him upwards into a lonely twist of sky and from whose eternity there was no escape but the plunge down towards the faraway houses and the little ribbons of roads, dead, just as his mother had been, long before he heard the shouting and screaming of the watching crowds. George saw friends of his begin to exhibit the mannerisms of despair. He pitied and feared. He examined himself in his dressing-room mirror. He beamed. He thought of Jennifer's wedding. He offered an imaginary Jennifer his arm. He remembered his mother's flying body. He thought about Beryl's birthday party. He drank imaginary champagne. He saw his office at the bank. He moved his imaginary body next door and placed it at the manager's desk. He beamed at an imaginary customer. The imaginary customer was respectful and awed and anxious. He put him at his ease. He looked back at the mirror. His beaming smile had left him.

So yes, he'd been forced to agree with Beryl, it hadn't been a very promising year. The question of the gone-forever managership interrupted both his sleep and his continuing cheerfulness. The dingyness of his room at the bank began to irritate him. He filled in a request slip for a red desk lamp. When, after two subsequent requests, it didn't arrive, he went to Ipswich and bought himself one. And it was while he was in Ipswich that he confronted the poster ('confronted' is precisely what George did: he stood absolutely still and stared at a photograph of sand, palm and gentle surf). 'Florida,' it said. 'Seven heavens under one sky.'

'Seven heavens?' Beryl had commented, disbelievingly, 'seven *figures* more likely.'

Beryl's pessimism, afflicting her more noticably after the menopause, served as an almost constant irritant to George's struggle with his own sanity. His desire to be loved by twenty-year-old women had perhaps less to do with sexual excitement than with his faith in the buoyancy of youth. Like safe, wide rivers, his love affairs kept his spirit afloat. He would never, as long as he kept company with firm flesh, be tempted off the roaring roller-coaster. In this way, he absolved himself of all his betrayals.

*

The shiny new golf clubs in their heavy white and red leather bag were, for George, the most perfect expression of an intention: a recently matured insurance policy, begun in 1962, would buy him and Beryl a Florida October. They would stay not in some anonymous Holiday Inn, but at the unique Palmetto Village Complex between Boca Raton and Boca West. Here, a short drive from Miami Beach, George planned to 'tee off for the experience of a lifetime', a phrase he coined the day he brought home the Palmetto brochure and which he used constantly in the months preceding the departure, finding that it captured perfectly both his hopes and the envy of his listeners (this last a necessity when he reflected that he had actually been saving for this trip for twenty years). The travel agent promised temperatures in the 80s. Onto the brochure picture of a couple eating breakfast under a parasol he had, in his mind, superimposed his own face. (A sense of loyalty made him try to superimpose Beryl's face opposite his own, but the woman under the parasol merely lost her identity, so that she was no longer the woman in the photograph, nor yet Beryl, but someone else, someone he could not actually put a face to.) He fondled the glinting golfing irons, felt their weight, putted balls across his sitting-room carpet, replaced them carefully and resisted any temptation to use them at the Woodbridge Golf Club. These were Florida irons. These were the tools of twenty years' grind. With these he would swing four thousand miles away, while England crept to winter under her soggy burden of leaves. With these he would decide whether he was ever coming back.

*

A black security guard, wearing a stetson and barracaded into a wooden booth examined the photographs of George and Beryl. He looked from the photographs to the back of the Chevrolet cab where they sat. 'Get out please, Sir,' he snapped.

The guard looked from George to the photograph and back to George. He saw a freckled, stocky man – the colouring of a Scot, the craggy build, perhaps, of a Welshman. Once powerfully blue and considered his best feature, George's eyes had faded, strangely, with time. His hair, once red, had faded too, not yet to white, but to an odd mixture of chestnut and grey, the colour of a certain breed of horse the name of which he always forgot. He was quite proud of his hair because it was still thick. He loved women to touch it.

'Can your wife get out please.'

Massively unsmiling, the guard astonished George. His bulk, his blackness, his hat, his abrupt commands: all were astonishing.

'He wants you to get out, Beryl.'

'Do we have to sign something, or something?'

'Dunno, dear. Careful of the clubs as you get out.'

The guard picked up Beryl's photograph. It showed a woman in a cardigan, hair newly set in a style resembling as nearly as possible the Queen's. (In his limited experience of English tourists, the security guard had noticed that a great number of women adopted this identical royal old-fashioned fashion.) Now, in a summer frock, Beryl's flesh looked very pale, almost blue-white at her ankles. In the blinding sunshine, she manoeuvred herself cautiously round the car and lined herself up beside George. The guard stared at them.

'Know the rules, Sir, Ma'am?'

'Sorry?' said George.

'No one gets in or out of the village without the security passes or a phone-in ID from a Palmetto resident. Day or evening guests are exempted, *pro*-viding they're with you, okay?'

'I don't think we'll be having guests . . .' began Beryl. 'We don't know anyone.'

'Pass expires last day of October,' the guard said with finality.

'What if we want to renew?' inquired George.

'Re-new?'

'Yes. If we decide . . .'

'Take minimum two IDs to the PVC Office . . .'

'PVC?'

'Palmetto Village Complex Office, 3125 Oranto Boulevard, Boca Raton. Two IDs minimum, plus apartment re-reservation documentation.'

It was all a bit of a jumble to me, said Beryl ten minutes later, as she slowly took in the details of the apartment, her home-to-be for a month of her life. But George wasn't listening. He was standing at a sliding window, gazing with awe at two smiling men in check trousers and white short-sleeved shirts embarking for the tenth hole on their motorised golf cart. George was open-jawed. No one had told him that the golf course would be spread out, like the Garden of Eden, in front of his veritable window.

'What about this, Beryl!' he exploded.

'I like the bathroom, George. Do come and see the bathroom . . .'

'Twenty-four hour round the clock bloody paradise!'

'What, dear?'

'It's right *here*. Right in front of our balcony!'

'What? The golf course?'

'Yes.'

'Do you think we're members automatically, being Palmetto residents?'

'Of course we are. It's one of the privileges. Golf and the swimming pool. Free to all Palmetto inmates.'

Beryl crossed the soft-carpeted room and stood next to George, looking out. As the two golfers drove off, a sudden wind frayed the inert palms and sang through the mosquito meshing. Beryl blew her nose. 'I don't expect those little carts are free' she said.

*

George woke with a feeling of joy he couldn't remember experiencing since he was twelve and sent one summer from a morbidly quiet home to a seaside scout camp in Cornwall.

He lay and admired the room. He sensed the different ways in which it had been designed with the privileged in mind: heavy drapes at the window, letting in no hint of the colossal day beginning outside them, wall-to-wall white louvered cupboards with heavy gold-plated knobs, built-in dressing alcove, complete with lace-covered tissue dispenser, additional makeup mirror and gilded ring tree (on which Beryl had hung her only ring, a faded bit of Victorian turquoise), heavy glass table burdened with heavy magazines and a piece of modern sculpture which George's unpractised eye had privately christened "Man Copulating With Hoop", chandelier style ceiling light, high pile white carpet, a framed bullfight poster, a set of eighteenth-century French prints, showing wigged aristocrats engaged in what seemed to be flirtation. It was worth it,

George whispered to himself, worth every penny just to have got this far.

His clock, re-set to US time, told him it was 7.10 a.m. Beryl slept her habitual hunched-up sleep, unvarying it seemed in any time zone. George crept to the bathroom, peed as quietly as he could (Florida lavatories seemed to echo less than English ones) and dressed quickly in brand-new lightweight trousers, holiday shirt and new canvas shoes. Picking up the apartment key, monumentally tagged to stop anyone pocketing it, he tiptoed out, pausing only to stare breathlessly at the quality of the light coming into the sitting room from across the golf course.

The Palmetto apartment buildings, though near to each other, were each arranged around their own careful garden. The grass was constantly watered and very green; in sculptured stone basins, shaded by palms, apologetic fountains sent feeble jets of water onto ferns and lilies. Planted among the oleander trees in each central courtyard was a marble map of the village. Gold lettering informed George YOU ARE HERE. Thanking the Palmetto planners for their foresight and helpfulness, George began to follow the memorised marble path to the circle marked GOLF COURSE ENTRY.

I am walking, he thought, with springy step. I slept a free sleep, uncluttered by any hint of nightmare. It's seven in the morning of my first day and already I've shaken England off like jumble sale clothes, just chucked it away, the better to breathe, the better to relax my shoulders, the better to tap a miraculous new energy located if I'm not wrong, or rather, beginning, at my groin and going through me like spring sap. And I am, extraordinarily, alone. It's as if, on this entire peninsular, no one is moving yet, unless it's the security guard, housed up in his booth, gun at the ready to protect me and all those asleep including Beryl from marauders and rapists and felons. A light wind is making me wish I'd brought along my pale blue C & A poloneck, but this is no doubt a dawn wind, very likely to die down as the sun hots up. Someone, I can now hear, is vacuuming the swimming pool. I dare say this is done regularly every morning to leave it jewel-bright for my pre-breakfast swim. If I was wise, I would pop into the pool complex to ascertain the temperature of the water . . .

A wagon, not unlike an enlarged version of the little golf

carts, was parked at the entrance to the swimming pool. On its immaculate sides was written PALMETTO GARDENING INC. and George now noticed that the vehicle was stocked with every variety of garden implement, including heavy yellow hoses. Nothing looked dirty. He recalled the rusting rural slum of his own garden shed and marvelled. Hardly any rain, of course he remembered, that would explain the absence of rust, but not the astonishing appearance of newness. A hoe looked as bright as his No. 2 iron.

Beside the wooden doorway to the pool was another marble map, again informing George, YOU ARE HERE. Wondering whether any resident of Palmetto had ever been lost anywhere in the village, he pushed open the door. The pool, roman-ended, was forty foot by eighteen. Gently moving the vacuum pole around its shallow end was a girl with long, colourless hair. She looked up immediately and stared at George. George stared. The girl was twenty. She wore skimpy, faded shorts and, above these, what looked to George like a home-stitched vest over ostentatiously milky breasts, damp nippled.

'Hi,' she said.

*

Beryl woke with astonishment and with the immediate certain-ty that she had a cold. Her throat was sore and her head ached. She called in the direction of the bathroom, 'George, are you up?' She waited. The only sound she could hear was a distant whooshing noise, perpetual, the Florida wind blowing in off the sea. Drawing back the heavy curtains, she blinked at the startling blue and green. The clarity of the morning made her wish that her own head would clear. She blamed this misfor-tune of a cold on altitude and climatic change.

'GOOD MORNING, PALMETTO RESIDENT!' said a plastic notice screwed to the kitchen wall. 'You are reminded that we do not serve breakfast as part of our four-star Palmetto Hospitality Agenda, but we hope you will make the fullest use of your kitchen facility. Your PALMETTO SHOP is located on Square 3 and will be delighted to sell you hot French bread, butter, jelly, tea, coffee, chocolate, milk, and of course Florida oranges. Meat for your griddle may also be obtained from your PALMETTO SHOP, should you prefer a substantial morning meal. The SHOP is open Monday through Sunday, eight to eight. Have a nice day.'

Beryl opened the fridge to see whether the previous Palmetto tenant had kindly left her anything in the way of breakfast materials, but the fridge was completely empty except for a cellophane-wrapped half bottle of Veuve Cliquot champagne, given free with every reservation of a week or longer. 'Drat it,' she commented, and, crossing back to the bedroom to dress for shopping, was startled by an unexpected and quite unfamiliar noise. The telephone was ringing.

Deciding that it must be George, and marvelling that he, who forgot important things with such regularity, had somehow memorised this number, she picked it up and said: 'George? What are you doing?'

'Beryl?' said a near sounding English voice, 'Brewer here. Brewer Smythe.'

Beryl thought, I've been astonished by every single thing since we got here and now here's Brewer Smythe astonishing me even more by ringing me when it was months ago that George wrote to Brewer and Monica, and as far as I know there's never been any reply from them.

'Heavens!' said Beryl.

'Surprised you, eh?'

'Well, to be honest, Brewer, I was just saying yesterday when we arrived that we didn't know anybody in Florida. And how wrong I was. I mean, I'd just forgotten about you. Isn't that terrible?'

'Oh, don't worry about trivial things like that, Beryl. How are you, anyway? And how's the old man?'

'Fine. We're fine. A bit jet-lagged, I mean I think I am because I seem to have got a cold, which I'm sure isn't usual. George has just popped out to . . . survey the golf course.'

'Well, listen. What about a plunge in at the deep end on your first day, eh?'

'Plunge in, Brewer?'

'Yes. Mr Weissmann wants me to take him up to River Kingdom for lunch. That's the best seafood place between here and Miami, and I've got you and George invited on the boat. Set off at 10.30-ish. Have cocktails on board. Get to River Kingdom at 12.30. George'll love it, Beryl.'

'Well, I don't know if I'm up to it, Brewer. I mean, with this cold . . .'

'Course you are. Best thing. Blow the cobwebs away.'

'Well, are you sure Mr Weissmann doesn't mind?'

'Absolutely! Told him George was not only an old friend, but a banker. He has the greatest respect for bankers.'

'It's very kind of you, Brewer . . .'

'Monica's coming. She's really looking forward to seeing you.'

'How is she?'

'Monica? Well, you wait till you see her! I tell you, Beryl, she's a changed woman since we moved here. If you say Woodbridge to Monica now, she can hardly remember what you're talking about!'

'Really?'

'Changed woman! But how are you and George finding it? Paradise, eh? Good first impressions, eh?'

Beryl hesitated. She realised the hesitation made her sound somehow ungrateful.

'I think it's all . . . extraordinary, Brewer. It'll take a bit of getting used to, but I'm sure once we do . . .'

'You'll never want to go home! Guarantee it, Beryl. Only to pack and get back here as fast as you can. You wait and see. But hats off to George for getting you here, anyway. So look, I'll be round to fetch you at 10.15. Oh, and Beryl, lunch is on us.'

Beryl sat down in the foodless kitchen. It's the kind of day, she thought, when I'm going to find it quite hard to believe anything that's happening.

*

'I'm new,' George had said to the girl.

'Yeah?'

She moved the pool vac with a steady, practised motion. George watched her. Her feet were bare. Her legs were long and tanned, the hairs on them golden and flat and unshaven.

'This is my first morning.'

'Yeah?'

'Yes. I was just doing a little, you know, recky.'

'Pool's okay. I prefer the ocean, though.'

The ocean. The thundering little word struck chords of magnificence in George's willing mind. He saw the girl walking bravely into breast-high surf, hair flying and wet, mouth parted on gleaming teeth. America, he thought. She is vigorous

America. He wanted to scoop her and the ocean into his lap.

'You've got the lot here, I'd say.'

'Pardon me?'

'Here. Climate, beaches, comfort, golf, ocean . . .'

'Yeah, it's okay. I miss the city, though.'

'The *city*? Do you?'

'Kind of. People want to learn in the city. Here, they're just all hipped on forgetting.'

George began to walk round the pool. Trying not to stare at the girl, he concentrated on its tiled blue depths.

'I suppose you do gardening as well? I saw your truck. If I may say so, I think the Palmetto gardens are most attractive.'

He heard her laugh. The young laughter made him feel suddenly old, and he stood still.

'I'm a qualified landscape architect,' said the girl. 'I got fired when I had my baby. Gardener was all I could get.'

'Um,' said George, uneasily, 'there's a lot of that happening.'

'Pardon me?'

'Well, that kind of thing. People over-qualified for the jobs they're doing.'

The girl didn't comment. George allowed himself to look up at her arm, slim but seemingly strong, moving the pool vac. The vigorous brown hair she chose to display in her armpit gave him a feeling both of excitement and of disquiet. Everything, he thought, in this country is utterly unfamiliar to me. I will go home an altered man.

'So you've got a baby?'

'Yeah. She's three months now.'

'A daughter? I have a daughter, Jennifer. She got married this year.'

'So you miss her, uhn?'

'Yes. In a way. My wife does.'

'Your wife with you out here?'

'Yes.'

'Great. Well have a nice stay.'

George recognised this as a dismissal. He began to walk slowly towards the pool exit, disappointed that the encounter had had a dull shape. Without identifying what, he knew that the minute he saw the girl he had hoped for something more. He stood, hands in his stiff new pockets, and stared at the roman end of the pool.

'Bet no one much gets up this early.' he said.

'No. We do, the gardeners and cleaners.'

'If I'm not being rude,' George began, 'I'd very much, I mean very much like to know –'

'Know what?'

'Your name.'

The girl held the pool vac still and stared accusingly at George.

'Want to fly me, or something?'

'What did you say?'

'Never mind. I don't give my name, though. Not to strangers.'

*

'The telephone went,' said a brightly dressed Beryl, who had decided bravely that she wouldn't mention her cold to George. 'It was Brewer.'

'Brewer?'

'Yes, Brewer. We're invited onto Mr Weissmann's boat for the day.'

'Which day?'

'Today. Now please let me have the key, George, and I'll go and buy us some bread and what they call jelly for breakfast.'

'How was Brewer?'

'Very cock-a-hoop. He said Monica was a changed woman.'

'Did you agree?'

'I haven't seen her yet, dear, so how could I agree or disagree?'

'No. To go on the boat.'

'Yes. It's very kind of Mr Weissmann.'

'It's our first day, Beryl.'

'Well, I know, but Brewer said there's a trip to some fish restaurant and I know you'd like that.'

'Suppose we can get in a game of golf this evening.'

'If we feel like it. I mean, after cocktails and lunch and all that, we may want a little sleep.'

'Oh I won't. We've only got a month, Beryl. We shouldn't waste a second.'

'Well, we'll see. I'll go and get the breakfast on Square 3, wherever that is.'

'Easy, dear. Just follow the map.'

When Beryl had gone, George opened the sliding window and sat down on the balcony under the white parasol. Here I am, he thought, like the man in the brochure. In the picture, though, there didn't seem to be any wind. Everything seemed hotter and calmer and much safer than it feels. Slightly breathless from what had been a long walk, he noticed in himself a mildly disturbing sense of unease, a feeling of fright. He slowed his breathing, took gulps of warm air. Careful never to lie to himself about his states of mind, he asked himself, was it the girl, her presence by the pool, her misunderstanding of an innocent, yes innocent question? Had the girl got in the way of contentment? He'd tried to forget her as he'd trod the lush turf of the Palmetto Golf Course, saying to himself she doesn't belong, she's a fugitive from the city, that's it, the Fugitive Kind, giving birth on Greyhound buses, breastfeeding on the freeway, in the subway, no matter where, never belonging with her provoking underarm hair, belonging nowhere, particularly not here, in a guarded village where no one passes without a pass, where the marble maps reassure you every few yards, YOU ARE HERE. Yet he hadn't been able to forget her. The girl and the great wind blowing from the east, they buffeted him and made him feel small.

George got up, crossed to the louvered bedroom cupboards and dragged out the leather bag of golf clubs. He carried them to the balcony and sat for a moment with his arms around them.

*

Brewer Smythe drove a Cadillac. George and Beryl sat beside him in the wide front seat, both wondering but not asking whether the car was Brewer's or Weissmann's.

Brewer was immensely fatter than when last glimpsed, trailing fatigue and failure around his Woodbridge boatyard. But he wore his new flesh proudly, like he might have worn a new suit, set it off with the whiteness of his naval shirt, topped it with a grinning, ruddy face and a naval-style cap gold-inscribed *Nadar III*. Body and uniform said, I've prospered. Freckles had formed on his arms so densely, they merged into a blotchy, chestnut coloured tan. On his wrist, an oversized platinum digital watch seemed put there as a reminder that here was a man to whom time had behaved kindly. Fifty-five now, this was Brewer's fourth year in Florida, working for the rich boat-owners of the most expensive waterways in the world, transforming years of worthless nautical knowledge into a sudden bonanza.

'Well, Monica's falling over herself!' said Brewer, simultaneously pressing a knob marked 'window lock' and another marked 'air'. 'Faces from Suffolk in our very own Boca Raton! It's hard to believe, honestly it is.'

'You look ever so well, Brewer,' said Beryl.

'Me? I'm in the pink. Never happier. Honestly. Best years of my life out here. You wait and see.'

'What's this Weissmann like?' asked George.

Brewer drew effortlessly into the fast lane of the freeway and accelerated.

'He's rich, George. I'd never seen wealth like his till I came out here. You wait till you see *Nadar*. And his house. Jesus! I'm not fooling when I say he's got a Picasso in his hallway.'

'Good to work for, is he?'

'Man of the world. Married three times. Knows how to treat people. We'd be nowhere, Mon and me, without someone like him.'

'What do you do for him exactly, Brewer?' asked Beryl. 'I mean, I know you're his kind of captain, but is all you do is look after his boat?'

'I provide a service, Beryl,' announced Brewer. 'I think today will give you a fair impression of the service I provide. Men like Weissmann, people in the art and business field, don't have the time or the knowledge for practicalities; they want leisure to run smoothly, you understand what I mean? So he relies on me. Total trust. Absolute round-the-clock responsibility. And that's what I'm paid for.'

Off the freeway after a few miles, the Cadillac was ambling now along a series of identical avenues of houses, low, detached and white, or built of sandstone blocks, each with a sloping front garden, tarmac driveway and wrought-iron gates leading to patios and swimming pools. Palms dwarfed the houses everywhere. 'You can travel,' Brewer informed George and Beryl, 'from your back garden to the ocean through the Florida canals. Unique in the world, and we've done it in *Nadar III*. Extraordinary, eh?'

'Cracking,' said George.

Their arrival at *Nadar*'s mooring was awkward. Monica, in

slacks and shocking-pink silk shirt and rattling with charm bracelets, mouthed an enthusiastic silent welcome to George and Beryl, while Weissmann, perched like a beady little penguin at the forward controls of the bulky boat, stared at them sullenly. Near to the thrice-married, sixty-year-old Weissmann was a fat, huge-eyed boy of ten, who also stared, sucking gum, with the brazen stare of the uniquely pampered.

Beryl looked up cautiously and smiled at Weissmann. His face remained impassive. Beryl turned to Brewer for help. Brewer, dwarfed by the boat, seemed momentarily to have lost both bulk and bounce.

'Mr Weissmann,' he said politely, 'may I present my good friends from England, Mr and Mrs Dawes – George and Beryl.'

'Welcome aboard,' said Weissmann, flatly. His accent was pure Germanic, almost unmixed with Yankee. He put a hirsute arm on the boy's rounded shoulder and announced, still unsmiling: 'This is my son, Daren. You see my boat is named *Nadar*. Daren is one half of *Nadar*. Daren is *Dar*. The *Na* piece of it comes from my wife's name. Nadia. Unfortunately, Nadia is in Paris, so Daren is stuck with his old Daddy, aren't you, Choots?'

'Choots' didn't reply at once, but continued to gaze blankly at George and Beryl.

'It's very kind of you, Mr Weissmann,' began Beryl.

'No, no,' said Weissmann, 'friends of Brewer's from England, this is the least we can do, eh Choots?'

'Daddy,' said Choots, 'are you going to pay for their lunch?'

*

'Do you want to handle her today, Mr Weissmann?' called Brewer from the aft controls, as he swung the boat out into the wide canal.

From the front cabin, where George and Beryl waited silently with Monica, you could just glimpse the enormous metal and plastic chair on the upper deck where Weissmann sat, a complex control panel laid out in front of him. Choots stood disconsolately beside him.

Monica whispered, 'Brewer has to be ever so careful. It's a new boat, you see, and Mr Weissmann hasn't quite got the hang.'

'I'll handle her,' Weissmann called back to Brewer, 'then when we get to River Kingdom, you take her in.'

'Okay, Sir. She's all yours, then. I'll do the cocktails.'

'Good. No cocktail for Choots today,' and here began a tremor of a smile in Weissmann's voice, 'he's too young.'

Brewer turned to George and Beryl who were now both looking at Monica. Monica was indeed a changed person. Like Brewer, she seemed to have undergone a colour metamorphosis. They remembered a faded, brown-shod woman with greying hair and an illusive, apologetic smile. What now confronted them was a blonde with shiny, tanned face, wearing Italian white sandals and azure eye shadow. The smile had broadened, found confidence. The voice, when she eventually began to talk to them, had taken on enough American vowel-richness to alter it greatly. It was, in fact, difficult to believe that this was Monica. Brewer put his arm round his wife and offered her proudly for inspection. 'Looking neat, eh? Looking terrific, isn't she?'

'I wouldn't have recognised you, Monica,' said Beryl.

Monica beamed, let Brewer smack a kiss on her blonde head.

'What can I say?' she said. 'That's what Florida does.'

'You look great, Mon,' said George.

'Thanks, George. Well, it's great to see you, isn't it, Brewer? And on your first day. You just wait till you've been here a week. You'll never want to go home.'

'So Brewer says,' said George.

'What's it to be?' asked Brewer, opening a polished drinks cabinet, 'bloody marys, whisky sours . . .?'

'Heavens,' said Beryl, 'we don't normally drink this early, do we George?'

'That's the whole point of it, Beryl,' said Brewer, 'to start doing what you don't usually do. We've learned that, haven't we, Monica? Only then will you get in tune with Florida life.'

'I'll have my usual,' said Monica.

'Oh, what's your usual?' asked Beryl.

'Make one for Beryl, Brewer,' said Monica, 'then she'll see.'

Every room and compartment on *Nadar III* appeared to have been designed to accommodate what George had heard was called Cocktail Hour. Little veneered glass holders were clamped to chair arms, recessed into walls, bolted even to the lavatory tiles. You could not move on *Nadar* without finding a convenient place to set down your drink. Noting this, George thought, being rich is the art of forethought. I am too random a person, despite my ability with figures, to predict accurately where I or my guests might want to set down their cocktails. Everything on this boat is in precisely the right place with regard to its function, but I have none of the skills I recognise in this kind of planning. He stared up at Weissmann's seat of power, wondered what it would be like to stare at it almost every day, as Brewer did, and to know that all one possessed emanated from there, from a German art dealer who was fond of bankers. He looked at Brewer, expertly shaking and mixing cocktails. He's grown fat, he thought suddenly, to protect himself. But then George berated himself for this idiotic tendency he'd failed to leave behind in England – his tendency to analyse and question and seek the comfort of certainties. It impedes, he thought, my positive response to whatever happens, and the only important thing, here, is to enjoy myself.

*

River Kingdom, a flat-roofed, blue-painted building with its own substantial mooring, was, George decided, rather like a fish theatre. Models of lobsters and crayfish and crabs and blue-fin sharks busked up the walls and across the ceiling, netting hung down in carefully arranged loops, tanks of living eels were spotlit, menus were like programmes: Act One, shrimp-crab-mussel-prawn-clam-oyster, Act Two, brill-striped bass-eel-mullet-lobster-shark fin and so on through a dramatis personae of water meat George had never in his life encountered. Waitresses in usherette black brought unasked-for salads as an overture to the meal. Outside the sun went in, as if the house lights had suddenly been turned down.

George was seated between Weissmann and Monica. Daren sat between his father and Brewer, which left the two women next to each other. But Weissmann, who had arranged the seating, had deliberately placed Beryl and Monica in seats where he wouldn't have to talk to them. Duty called on him to tolerate his captain and his friend as lunch guests, but not their wives. The elaborate courtesies he reserved for the women of his own elite weren't available for the likes of Beryl: patronage went only so far.

Beryl and Monica talked about England and Suffolk in particular and Woodbridge and Wakelin All Saints. At one moment, George heard Monica say, 'I've forgotten to ask him, I suppose George is manager by now?' and cast an anxious look at Beryl, who seemed defeated both by her gigantic shark steak and by the question. He looked away.

'So,' said Weissmann, turning an indifferent eye upon George, 'you like America.'

This was neither question nor statement, but something in between. George looked at Brewer, who was grinning encouragingly, then coughed.

'It's our first time,' he said. 'We flew from Gatwick yesterday. I'm quite surprised by everything I've seen.'

'Surprised? In what way surprised?'

'Oh, I don't know,' said George, 'it's very hard to pinpoint precisely where the differences occur. Everything seems unlike England in a way I can't yet explain. I thought it might just be a question of size and climate, but it isn't.'

'Well,' said Weissmann, portentously, 'this is the United States.'

'Right, Sir!' said Brewer. 'I've been saying to George, now that he's here, he'll never want to go back. We haven't. We've never had a moment's regret.'

'You like Europe?' asked Weissmann, blackly. And George felt an irritating panic rise in him. Europe. The images conjured by Weissmann's use of the word, the images to which he was expected to respond, were all, all as alien to George as words like quatrocento and surréaliste and schadenfreude and Auschwitz. Weissmann, American, Jew, *knew* 'Europe'; George, Englishman and part of Europe, did not.

'I'm fond of the country,' said George, taking up the wine one of the usherettes had poured for him.

'Which country?' said Weissmann.

'The countryside,' stammered George, 'the countryside of England.'

'But Brewer said you were a banker.'

'Yes. I am. I'm with Mercantile and General.'

'In the City, no?'

'What, London? Oh no, I'm not in London.'

'So you're not a real banker, then.'

George was saved from having to comment on his own

reality by the nagging of Choots who, with the underwater world spread out for his delectation, had ordered cold roast beef and pickles.

'This isn't nice, Daddy,' said Choots.

'No?' said Weissmann.

'No.'

'Why did you choose it, then?'

'I didn't choose it. Brewer chose it for me.'

Brewer smiled. 'It's what he asked for, Sir.'

'Don't eat it,' Weissmann said, 'give it to Brewer.'

Choots went off to the serve-yourself sweet table and helped himself to a wedge of chocolate gateau. Brewer good-naturedly crammed the thick slices of red beef onto his lobster plateau and proceeded to eat both simultaneously.

Weissmann smiled.

'He's a good man, Brewer, your friend,' he said to George, 'he does what I ask, eh Brewer?'

'Yes, Sir!'

'I spoil my son, you are thinking. In Europe, children are not spoiled. I was not spoiled. I was kicked and bullied. Now, I'm the one with the boots, you see? But not for my son. He will have what he wants because I am too old to be a good father and this is punishment enough. So you're not really a banker?'

George found Weissmann's twists and turns of thought vexing; he invited you to enter a conversation, then left you no room to participate in it.

'I've been in banking all my life,' said George quietly.

'You know money?'

This was like the Europe question. It reverberated cavernously with meaning inaccessible to the likes of George. He sighed. This was the first sigh he had heard himself breathe since landing at Miami airport. To his own astonishment, he heard himself say angrily, 'I know, Mr Weissmann, what this holiday is costing me.'

*

Monica's special cocktail hadn't agreed with Beryl's stomach. Back at Palmetto, she was lying in the large bed (lying, she realised, rather stiff and straight so as not to rumple the sheets an unseen maid had so carefully smoothed) feeling pale and drowsy. George, perched by the Man Copulating With Hoop, stared anxiously at his wife.

'Why don't you go off and have a game of golf, George?' Beryl suggested.

George smiled. 'I can't play with myself, Beryl.'

Beryl placed her two hands comfortingly on her stomach and tried to breathe deeply. A novice at the Wakelin All Saints Yoga for Beginners, she had learned that pain can be relieved by mind control allied to correct breathing.

'I'm terribly sorry, George. I don't know whether it was the shark or Monica's cocktail, or just simply me. I didn't take to that Weissmann, did you?'

'Just rest, Beryl.'

'I'm alright to talk. I wouldn't want to be Brewer, would you?'

'He's changed.'

'I wouldn't want to be at the beck and call of a spoilt person like that.'

'Brewer doesn't seem to mind. And anyway, we don't know him, Beryl. I expect art connoisseurs are a difficult lot.'

'Do go and play golf, dear. I'm sure you'll find someone to give you a game.'

George got up and crossed to the bed. 'Going to have a bit of a sleep, then, are you?'

'I think I will.'

'Good boat, wasn't it? Imagine owning that.'

'Too powerful for me. Too built up.'

'Built up?'

'Well, it was just one deck put on top of another, put on top of another, wasn't it? No line.'

George looked fondly at Beryl. There were moments – not very many – when his abiding sense of his wife as a humdrum woman suddenly parted like the Red Sea and another (sensitive, sharp-witted) Beryl came striding through. This was one such moment.

'Rest, love,' he said gently, and touched her forehead with his finger, as if offering her a benediction.

Beryl closed her eyes and seemed, in that instant, asleep. George tiptoed out of the room and quietly closed the door. He walked to the balcony window of the sitting room and stared longingly at the golf course. Above it, behind the palms, the sky was flat and grey – a peculiarly English sky – and the wind was blowing hard. The sun hadn't been seen after they'd sat down to lunch at River Kingdom, and the journey home through choppy water had been disagreeable. Weissmann had left the boat with only a nod to George and Beryl, saying anxiously to Brewer, 'There may be a storm. Make sure the mooring is very safe.'

George had no sense of any impending storm, but the golf course was clearly deserted. Palmetto people only played golf in the sunshine. Or else they knew that a storm was coming, they read signs that George was unable to decipher, bought their evening griddle steaks and drew their heavy curtains.

It was warm in the room. George opened the sliding balcony window. The parasol had been closed and only the fringe moved slightly with the wind. George sat down at the table and rubbed his eyes. Too much has happened, he thought, in the space of time I had reserved only for an arrival. The extraordinary early morning joy, the girl with her damp breasts and her disdain, the ride in the Cadillac, the boat trip, lunch, Choots, tiny glimpses into worlds and lives he would never know; he was left with a feeling of stifling confusion. 'I need time,' he said aloud, 'I need more time.'

He began to soothe himself with the comfort of the coming days and weeks. Hot, quiet days spent with Beryl on the golf course, lunches at the pool, shopping for gifts for Jennifer in the famous shopping malls, a day trip to Miami beach . . .

George sat back, folded his arms. He was tired, he now recognised. The time change had suddenly hit him. He closed his eyes, heard the wind fill his head. Why had no one mentioned the presence of the wind? Then, on the edge of sleep, he heard his own voice announce with sudden and absolute certainty: 'They're gone.' His eyes snapped open. He stared down, tracing each concrete foot of the balcony on which he sat. He felt nauseous, drained. He ran a moist hand through his thick hair. 'They're gone.'

He got up. The maid had moved them, had she? She had put them back in the louvered cupboard or propped them up by the door? He crossed the sitting room, entered the kitchen. They weren't by the door, they weren't in the kitchen. He was sweating now, drenched in sweat. He would have to wake Beryl or risk waking her by opening the wardrobes. He opened the bedroom door quietly. Beryl was asleep, nose gasping at the ceiling. George moved stealthily to the cupboards, pulled them wide open, gazed at his lightweight clothes, Beryl's cotton dresses, their mingled pile of new shoes, recognising that what he was feeling was fear, a drenching of fear such as he couldn't remember since, as a timid boy, the secret mouldering apple store in his toy cupboard had been crushed to pulp by his mother's suicidal rage, dinky cars and lead soldiers, cigarette cards and painted matchboxes lying ruined and stained in brown rot.

'Beryl . . .' he said tightly.

Beryl moved but slept on, snoring gravely.

'Beryl . . .' George heard the choke in his voice and knew it for a suppressed scream. 'Someone has stolen my golf clubs.'

Beryl didn't move, but opened a bleary eye and looked at her husband. 'George,' she said, alarmed, 'are you crying?'

*

The black security guard shifted his massive frame on the high backed chair and turned towards the chain-locked side door of his booth on which George had tremblingly knocked.

'Come round to the window!' yelled the guard. He touched his gun with a wide finger, let a signal for dangerous and immediate action ripple through his chest and arms. George's rowan head appeared at the booth glass.

'Can I see your pass, Sir?'

George fumbled for his wallet, into which he had carefully put his pass and Beryl's.

'I've come to report a theft . . .' began George.

'Security pass, please,' snapped the guard.

George laid the pass on the little counter, wanted to comment that the guard had seen him not one hour ago as Brewer drove them home in the Cadillac, but refrained from saying this and waited patiently while the guard examined his (by now familiar, surely?) photograph inside its piece of transparent plastic.

'Theft, you said?'

'Yes.' George cleared his throat. 'I left my golf clubs on my balcony . . .'

'We don't get theft at Palmetto. You better have another search.'

'I have searched. The golf clubs are not in my apartment.'

'You got insurance?'

'Yes. I have a policy with Norwich Union . . .'

'Okay, this is one for the PVC Office. Take minimum two IDs down to 3125 Oranto Boulevard and state the exact nature and time of the theft. All unsecured property, however, is disclaimed for responsibility purposes by Palmetto Village Security and balcony property is deemed unsecured for this purpose.'

'What?' said George.

'All unsecured, that is open or balcony property is *dis*-claimed for responsibility purposes by PV Security.'

'You mean Palmetto is not responsible?'

'You got it.'

'Then I don't see the point of these passes and all the security regulations. If you can just let a thief walk in and steal my golf clubs . . .'

'You tell the PVC Office, Sir.'

'And what will they do?'

'You got two IDs?'

'Yes. What will the Palmetto Office do?'

'Question you, Sir.'

'Question *me*! Look, I was out all day. I returned at four thirty p.m. to find my clubs missing. That's all I can tell them. But I am not exaggerating when I say that those clubs cost me almost a month's salary. I want them found and the thief caught!'

George realised that he was shouting. Fatigue, he thought, and fear have made me deaf to my own voice. The guard was staring at him with interest, the stare of a man watching a zoo-caged animal. He avoided the stare and turned to walk away.

Behind him the PALMETTO GARDENING van had appeared like an apparition, soundless and unseen. George stopped and stared at it. His hand, still clutching his wallet, was shaking. The girl tugged on the hand brake, unfolded her willowy body from the cart and strode to the booth. In the strong wind, her hair was whipped around her face, hiding it from George. 'Everything conspires,' he heard himself whisper, not knowing precisely what he meant. He watched without moving as the girl waved her security pass at the guard, heard the guard say, 'Hi, Cindy. Get home before the storm, Uhn?' George's eyes moved to the skimpy vest. He saw that her nipples were dry.

'Hello,' he said quietly.

The girl turned. The wind caught her hair, lifting it back from her face. She reached up and held the hair and looked down at George. He noticed for the first time how very tall she was.

'Oh . . .' she said.

George clutched his wallet, willed his body to stop shaking. I'm ill, he thought, and the girl began it. He tried to smile at her. Rested, refreshed and at peace with himself – on some other day – he could have said, 'Don't misunderstand the kind of man I am. I only asked your name because I prefer everything to be known and unambiguous. Although I find you extraordinary and might allow myself the luxury of erotic fantasising around your milky breasts and your eyes as grey as the sky, I would never presume, that is I would never be so vain as to suppose you would give me anything of yourself . . .' Instead, he said nothing at all, saw the girl glance anxiously from him to the cart full of tools to the guard who was smiling at her, his massive presence transfigured by the smile.

'Not many takers,' mumbled George.

'Pardon me?' said the girl quickly.

'For the pool,' said George, indicating the dense cloud above them.

'Oh,' said the girl, 'I guess not.'

And she was gone, springing back into the cart, waving at the guard, who waved back, and driving off down the clean grey road that led to the freeway.

*

The storm came rolling in on a sky blacker than dusk. Beryl made tea. The pains in her stomach came and went.

George sat on the sofa and listened to the vast, moving sheets of rain exploding against the sliding windows, felt the building shudder in the body of the wind.

Two thoughts chased each other round his brain which felt squeezed and bruised: Weissmann's boat is adrift and sinking in the storm; the girl stole my golf clubs, stowed them and hid

132

them among her shiny garden tools, and will sell them to buy things for her baby . . .

Beryl came in and looked at George. 'Change your mind and have some tea, George,' she said.

But no, he didn't want tea. 'I'm beginning to think, Beryl,' he said, 'that we never should have come.'

A sudden spasm of pain rose in Beryl's stomach and she sat down on the sofa beside George with an ungainly bump.

'Don't be silly, dear,' she said with as much energy as her voice could muster, 'you're usually the optimist.'

'It was one of the gardeners,' said George.

'One of the gardeners what?'

'Stole my golf clubs.'

'I haven't seen any gardeners.'

'I have. Women.'

'Well,' said Beryl, placatingly, 'as soon as the storm's over – tomorrow morning – we'll go down to the Palmetto Office and get it all sorted out.'

She understands nothing, thought George, nothing, *nothing*. Things cannot now be 'sorted out' because they are irrevocably altered. I have, in no more than twenty-four hours, encountered worlds that I do not understand. The girl is one world, the girl and her crime and the guard who is not interested that a crime has been committed against me. The other world is Weissmann, whose voice challenged me, yes challenged me at the entrance to some cave or echoey place and in that cave were all the songs and sufferings of a continent and the rich, rich owners of the wealth of that continent that I do not, nor will ever possess nor understand. I have, in a trice, simply understood my own profound and unchangeable insignificance.

Answering voices placated, denied: you said you wanted 'recovery from mediocrity'. You cannot 'recover from mediocrity' unless you understand the nature of that mediocrity. You have now begun to understand. At sixty, it's not too late to make a start, just as autumn is not merely a dying off, but as the leaves fly, hard new buds form already and wait for April . . .

'I suppose,' said Beryl suddenly, 'we should have bought steak or something for the griddle. You'll be hungry later on.'

But they weren't hungry and didn't eat. The wind howled

and screamed in the mosquito wire. On the balcony, the table fell over and the parasol went flying off into the night like a javelin. The pain in Beryl lessened and she got out the cards. George agreed blankly to play Gin Rummy and silently won every round till the lights went out and Beryl gave a little scream. Almost simultaneously, the telephone rang and George fumbled his slow and terrified way to the kitchen to answer it. Beryl found a table lighter, which clicked up a minute yellow flame. Holding this, she came and stood by George's side.

The voice on the line sounded far away. Jennifer, thought George, it's Jennifer. Something's happened in England.

'Jen?'

'What?' said the voice.

'Is that you, Jen? This is Dad.'

'George? It's Monica.'

'Oh, Monica . . .'

'Brewer thought we ought to ring, just to make sure you're okay. It's quite a bad storm. Have your lights gone?'

'Yes. They just went.'

'We're still okay in Boca Raton. Poor you. What a welcome to Florida! Would you like Brewer to come over and get you in the car?'

'No, no,' said George, 'we're fine. But what about the boat?'

'The boat?'

'Weissmann's boat. It'll be adrift, won't it?'

'Well, I don't think so, George. Why should it be?'

'In the storm . . .'

'Brewer will have taken care of it.'

'I think it's gone, Monica. I think it's drifting and breaking . . .'

There was a long silence at Monica's end of the telephone. George was aware that he was breathing petrified shallow breaths. Beryl's face, lit by the tiny lighter flame, stared at him aghast. She reached out and gently took the telephone receiver from him.

'Monica,' she said, 'this is Beryl.'

'Oh, Beryl,' said Monica, relieved, 'what's the matter with George? Is he afraid of the storm?'

'No,' said Beryl, 'I don't think it's that.'

'What's happened, Beryl?'

'Well, he's just a bit upset because his golf clubs have been stolen.'

'*Stolen?* At Palmetto? It's not possible, Beryl. Palmetto's like Fort Knox.'

'Well, I know, but there you are. He left them on the balcony and they're gone. They were brand new.'

'Is he certain, Beryl? Has he looked everywhere?'

'Oh yes. Everywhere.'

'Well, I'm amazed. I never heard of anyone stealing anything at Palmetto . . .'

'No. Well, I dare say there's always a first time.'

'Anyway, tell him not to worry. He can have Brewer's. Brewer hardly plays any more. No, honestly, he's too busy with Weissmann's empire. I'll bring them round in the morning.'

*

With Brewer's golf clubs, scarcely less new and shiny than his own, and with the passing of the storm, the month began to settle down. The parasol lost in the storm was replaced, and religiously every morning George and Beryl breakfasted under it, like the people in the Palmetto brochure.

They were never again invited aboard Weissmann's boat, nor did they glimpse the Picasso in his hallway. But they spent some time in the bungalow Brewer and Monica had recently bought at Boca Raton, struggling to find the superlatives with which to admire Brewer's Seafarer Cocktail Cabinet, fitted out with mock compasses and other nautical pieces of brass entirely unfamiliar to them, and Monica's polystyrene rock, dyed green and brown (like army camouflage, George noted privately) over which a recycled waterfall trickled continuously into a tiny circular swimming pool.

'Doesn't it all make you want to stay for ever?' said Monica one morning to Beryl, as they wandered the expensive shopping malls in search of presents for Jennifer and her new husband. Beryl caught a glimpse of herself in the shop window they were passing; her skin was lightly tanned, her hair had been reshaped by Monica's pet hairdresser, Giani, obliterating all its former resemblance to the Queen's.

'Well, I think I've changed,' said Beryl, 'and that's probably a good thing. I think at our time in life, you need a little jolt like this – something different – to put everything in perspective. But George and I are happiest where we are. I don't think Florida is quite right for us, not like it's been right for you and Brewer.'

'But Wakelin All Saints, Beryl, it's such a backward little place.'

'Yes, it is. Oh, I know that.'

'And you said George won't even get to be manager. Now, I'm sure Mr Weissmann has strings enough out here to fix George up with something. I mean, money isn't a dirty word out here like it is in England. And if you're in money, Beryl, as George is . . .'

'Oh, he's not "in" it, Monica. I think to be "in" money, you've got to have some, and George has never had any, only his salary.'

'Well, he knows money.'

'No. I don't think he "knows" it, either. He just went into the bank because he thought it would be safe.'

'Safe? Safe from what?'

'Oh, you know, Monica. Sort of from the world.'

*

The world spins faster here, George decided. Storms and hurricanes arrive in moments; flowers on the Palmetto squares come out and die in a day; by the pool, my towel is dry and stiff in half an hour. And people disappear. The girl. Weissmann. I look for the girl every day. I've seen her little cart dozens of times, but she's never in it or near it. One morning, I woke early and thought I was lying on her, my mouth on her milky breasts, my hand holding fast to her hair, like a rope. I got up and went to look for her. But I found a young man vacuuming the pool and she was nowhere. Probably she's run away, knowing she committed a crime.

And Weissmann? Brewer has a photograph of the man shaking hands with President Reagan. Brewer sees Weissmann every day. Choots is dumped on Monica, who makes him apple pie. But Choots never addresses one word to me. We had our audience on the first day and now we're forgotten, dismissed. We hire a dumpy cruiser one afternoon and pass *Nadar III*. Brewer waves. Weissmann, from his perched-up control panel, stares at us like complete strangers.

Jennifer wrote from England: 'I don't believe we've had such a glorious autumn in Suffolk since 1976. We've been mushrooming before breakfast three or four times, and the misty, sunny early mornings are superb. No rain for a couple of weeks now and an incredible blackberry crop. Shame you're missing it, but trust the Florida sun compensates . . .'

So the month drifted to its end. Beryl sorted and wrapped the presents she had bought and acquired a lightweight canvas bag in which to carry them home. George took photographs hastily, badly, a last-minute snapping of palm and balcony and pool and river bungalow, then a final indoor sequence with Beryl moving obediently from room to room.

'We should have thought about pictures earlier on, George,' said Beryl, 'I mean, pictures are half of it, aren't they?'

'Half of what, dear?'

'It. The experience. So you don't forget it.'

'Don't worry, Beryl. I won't forget it.'

Beryl was seated on the velvet pile couch, tanned legs crossed, hair newly set (Giani had cut the front into a rigid fringe, which made Beryl look more severe – and more intelligent – than she was), and George was backing nearer and nearer to a line of bookshelves crammed with unread, leather-bound volumes inscribed 'Weatherburns Classic Series'.

'Watch out for the books,' said Beryl.

'I want to get you in, and just a suggestion of the balcony view . . .'

George's bottom rammed the bookcase. Beryl's mouth, composed primly for the photograph, fell open as she saw George and the books behind him begin to turn and revolve and finally disappear almost out of sight into a dark hole in the wall.

'George!' she yelped.

George tipped. The camera was jolted out of his hand and fell to the ground. He clutched at the books, recovered his balance, found himself inside a clean cupboard, smelling of airwick, completely empty except for one bulky, familiar object, propped up in a corner, safe, intact and still radiating its extraordinary newness – his bag of golf clubs.

Beryl was now at George's side. 'My God, George,' she said, 'you looked like a person on the Paul Daniels Magic Show!'

'Look,' said George, 'just look.'

George picked up the camera and handed it to Beryl. He reached out for the leather strap of the golfing bag, hauled the bag out into the room, and let the false cupboard door revolve back into place behind him. Beryl said nothing, just watched as George touched the clubs in disbelief, examining each one, brushing a thin film of dust from the bag.

'My God!' he said.

'Well . . .' said Beryl.

Then George sighed, let the bag fall, walked very slowly to the balcony window and stared out. There was no wind on this day. The palm leaves hung limp and dry, the fringe of the parasol wasn't moving. Gentle, tropical air filled the room with warmth, the sun dappled it with sprigs of bright light. In two days, George thought, we will be in Suffolk and the calendar on my office wall will say November.

'At least we found them,' said Beryl.

'Yes,' said George quietly.

'Now we can go back with everything we came with.'

'Yes,' said George, but smiled a wide, astonished smile that Beryl never saw. She's wrong, he thought. We won't go back to England with all that we carried with us to America. There's a part of me which has been replaced.

The Stately Roller Coaster

I always say to the press, if you want me to blab, send me a pretty woman. You'll do. How old are you? Twenty-eight? You're not more than thirty, are you? Got a family, have you? Figure like Eleanor Roosevelt when she was thirty. Nice breasts. But too tall. How tall are you? Five ten? If more women had good breasts, they wouldn't need brassières. Can't stand to see the things curdling round their waists! One in seventeen of you get breast cancer. Know that, did you? I read it somewhere. P'raps you wrote it in your newspaper. One in seventeen.

That's it. You sit there. Lady Bressingham used to like that chair. My wife. She used to perch there and pat the dogs. Potty about those dogs! Let them clamber all over her, kiss their faces. She prefered them to our daughter. Women! Mothers, the lot of you. But my wife wanted to be mother to the spaniels. Let them into her bed. Turfed me out. Shooed me out into the dressing room and called to the dogs: Chuppy, Bimsie, Mac! Mac was short for Macassar. Lady Bressingham had an experience in Macassar, so she called the bloody dog after it.

Nice view from that chair. Think so? Used to be a bowl of flowers in front of the window, on that marquetry table. You could look out beyond the flowers if you wanted, or just look *at* the flowers. Lady Bressingham always looked *at* the flowers. Quite often she'd get up in the middle of a sentence and go and fiddle about with the flowers, rearranging them. But if I ever sit there, I look out of the window.

See the cedars? Planted by Gordon of Khartoum when he stayed here. Odd fellow, Gordon, they say. Mad as a hatter! The East does that – and the heat. If Lady Bressingham had stayed in Macassar, she'd have gone potty. But the cedars are jolly good. I like them. That was where it was going to begin – just beyond the cedars, just far enough so you couldn't see it if you sat in that chair. Can't remember the layout exactly, but I know the funfair was going to start there. Want to see the plans? Got them somewhere. Somebody called Curry did them: landscape man. Said he was 'in' with the county council. Said there'd be no fiddle-faddle. Formality, he said, just a formality. But he was wrong. Had to go m'self, in the end, to see the council people. Half of them women. First meeting we had I was told the toilet provision was inadequate.

Like a glass of sherry? Bloody cold, these winters. Told Mrs Baxter to light the fire early today, but she didn't. Chuck another log on, will you? Pull the chair nearer, if you like. Lovely smile, you've got. Always thought newspaper people were a humourless lot. Lovely smile and breasts. Tell at a glance you're a hit with the chaps. Children, have you? Husband? Did I ask you that? Can't remember a damn thing these days. Lucky man whoever he is. Sherry's behind you. Help yourself.

Tell you a bit about the place, shall I? Built 1612. High Jacobean. Been in my family since 1789. Passed to the Bressinghams from the Villiers via the female line. Called Villiers Hall till 1901. Name changed by my father after the death of the Queen. Bressingham suits it better: stronger word. Lived here most of my life. Got to know it as a boy. Knew every inch of it then. Every birdsnest. No wireless. No TV then. You made your own life up. We had cricket out there on the lawn. And a camp in the spinney. Made a tree house with my cousins. Called it The Flat.

Curry wanted to chop down part of the spinney, stick the aviary there. I said no. I said, put the aviary where Lady Bressingham's rose garden used to be and stick the bloody toilets behind it. Then you'd have had a walkway straight from the aviary to the funfair. It made sense. You can let a spinney go wild and it's still a spinney, but rose gardens won't do unless they're tidy. Hate rose gardens, anyway! Tea roses! Disgusting fatty blobs. Don't like them, do you? Well, it's all overgrown anyway. Covered in convolvulus. Not worth saving. I'd have liked to hear parakeets there. Much better idea. So I convinced Curry. And I told poor old Flannery, my head gardener, just forget about Lady Bressingham's rose garden, Flannery, let it go, let the weeds get it, because that's where the aviary's going to be. He's older than me, Flannery. Live long, the Irish, if they don't kill each other. But he's getting like the house now: corners falling off him!

Blabbing enough for you, am I? Saying the right things? Tell you the best thing I thought up with Curry – the lion pit! We were going to have lions anyway, but I said, why not a pit? Get a lion-tamer – someone who'll make the brutes go docile – dress him in an anorak, give him a folding pushchair to hold, make him look like a one-parent family, then throw him in. Gladiator of the Week, we'd call it – every Sunday, sharp at three. Curry wasn't keen. Said we'd be contravening some Protection of the Public act, but I said, Curry, I know a good idea when I smell one. Take feeding time at any zoo across the country; it's the danger element people are dribbling for: the man going into the cage with the raw meat. And the trick was, they wouldn't know he was a lion tamer. I love tricks. They'd think the man was a social worker.

Never liked the winter. Gets dark too early. Sherry keeps me going. Top me up, will you? Nice ankles you've got, too. Remind me a bit of Daphne. Got a son have you? Daphne had a son. Can't remember the boy's name. Derek or Daren or something. Shouldn't be talking about any of that anyway. Often think Lady Bressingham's listening in from the Quinta San José – if she's still alive. We don't communicate, you see. She's there in the Quinta San José near Lisboa as she calls it. And I'm here. Dreadful name, Daphne. Don't you agree? Terribly common name. Daff, I called her. Make me a naughty boy, Daff! Lock the bloody door and get hold of me quickly! Sixty-two I was when Daphne came here, and randy as a trick cyclist. God, I was randy! Hadn't had sex for years with Lady Bressingham, but when Daff arrived I couldn't control myself. Like a sixteen year-old, I was. Called it charvering when I was young. Odd bloody word for it. Day and night I'd dream of it – in my Bentley, down at the spinney, on the floor behind this bloody desk – charvering Daff. Don't print it, will you? Not meant to blab about any of that, but my God, it's lonely here. That's why I was all for the funfair. And the lions, and the aviary. Bring a bit of life in. Friends of mine said, don't do it, old man. Ruin Bressingham, you will, destroy its character.

But I said what the bloody good's character when the place is crumbling? I'll show you round when we've had the sherry. You can see for yourself what needs doing. Hasn't been touched, any of it, since Lady Bressingham left for Portugal. No money. Sold off a hundred acres to buy Lady Bressingham the Quinta San José. I heard she grows oranges. Mac must be dead by now. But I'd know if my wife was dead, I dare say. Some letter in Portugoose. Have solicitors out there, don't they? Lady Bressingham's name was Fidelity Belcher, before I got her. I seem to choose women with disagreeable names.

Like it on your newspaper, do you? Interesting life? On the road a lot, chasing scandals and people with breast cancer? They loathe a scandal in these parts. Want life to run flat, like a motorway. But I don't agree. I've always liked ups and downs. Look like a stick-in-the-mud, I know that, but I was the one who thought up the lion pit. It's the council who won't play. Curry said point nought nought fiddle-faddle, but what do we get in the end? Vetoes. You write that down, young woman. You put, 'Lord Bressingham, 75, owner of Bressingham Hall, is being denied his chance to confront the world of today.'

My daughter would have approved. I thought of writing to her, to get her to come and talk some sense into the county council, but I don't know where she lives. The last I heard she was in Hackney. I grew up thinking all the poor of the nation lived in Hackney. Too bloody poor to breathe the sooty air! In the war, they sent evacuees out from Hackney, but we never took any in. Lady Bressingham disliked children. If they'd evacuated dogs, we'd have been over-run! We'd have had open house! Funny woman, Fidelity Belcher. Often hoped she'd tell me what happened in Macassar. Something damned odd. Something she never forgot. She's probably going round her orange trees in her sunhat, this very afternoon, remembering Macassar. Imagine that! My daughter could be with her, but I doubt it. She didn't like us much, either one of us. Left us the minute she could. Lived with an Indian in Hackney. I said okay, good for you, no harm done, forgive and forget. I'm a tolerant man for a Peer. House of Lords is jam-packed with intolerant men, but I'm not among them. I said, bring Simon to Bressingham. He was called Simon, this Indian chap, not Vindaloo or Biriani, as you might expect. Simon. So I said, you bring him down and we'll kill the fatted calf! Forgot calves are sacred! Put my foot right in it there, eh? No harm intended. But she never forgave me. Worse than that, she tried to punish me.

Ever had children? Didn't ask you before, did I? Daff had a son. I wrote to Daff when this funfair scheme got going, took the liberty of reminding her of certain afternoons in my Bentley, asked her to come and see me and see Curry's plans. But I never heard a word. Shame, really. Beautiful buttocks, Daff had. Marvellous little fanny. Don't mind me talking like this, do you? Open-minded girl, are you? I'd have married Daff but for Lady Bressingham's Catholicism. Daphne was willing. I was a very potent man at sixty-two. She used to scream and tear at me. *Women*! My wife in bed with the dogs; Daff yelling her head off in the back of the Bentley! I thought my life had gone potty. No, I did. She was thirty-four. Not much older than you. Marriage hadn't worked. Left landed with her son. Came to me as a secretary. Had me going the minute I clapped eyes on her. I was well endowed then. I banged her all the time, better than an undergraduate. And she wanted me to marry her. She pleaded. So I thought, why not? What a wife to get at sixty-two! My God, I thought, my life's going to be a bloody miracle. So I went to Lady Bressingham. She was in bed with Bimsie and Mac, tickling their tummies. I sat on her bed and said, I'm in love with Daphne and Daphne's in love with me and I want a divorce. She was in her nightie. She said, pass me my bedjacket. So I gave her the bedjacket and she said, *never*.

There was a stink in the village, I can tell you. Lady Bressingham told them all – all the servants, all our friends, even the tradesmen and shopkeepers – my husband is unfaithful to me: my husband is betraying his name and mine. And poor Daff just couldn't take it. Those lovely screams of hers turned to hysteria. I did my level best to comfort her. I said, Daff, I may not be able to marry you, but I'll leave Bressingham and live with you in a flat. But no, she wanted marriage and that was that. She told me she was pregnant. What a to-do! Thought Bressingham would fall down round my ears! Never heard parakeets screech like Lady Bressingham screeched then. She began to break things, too. China ornaments. Vases. Hundreds of pounds she must have smashed. Terrifying! Then she went away. To Lisboa as she calls it.

Just by the by though, all that. The filling in life's pie – the colourful part. Most people hide those bits. But I'm quite fond of colour. I said to Curry, if we've got to provide toilets, let's do them orange and red striped like circus tents, let's make a feature of them. And if we're going to have a funfair, let's for heavens' sake have a good one, with fast machinery and all the thrills. I think I overdid it. Got carried away. But don't tell me people wouldn't have liked it. And the lion pit. Cracking idea. Better than anything Bath has at Longleat. Outdo 'em all!

Lovely view from that chair, don't you think? Like it, do you? I agree. But if it all goes on crumbling and sinking, you won't be able to sit there any more. They'll have to pull the old house down. Stick me in some geriatric establishment. Breaks my heart. A flat with Daff I wouldn't have minded. Far from it. But I dislike institutions. People fart a lot in institutions. Top me up, will you? Plenty more sherry in the cellar. Never run short of that. Don't suppose you could track my daughter down, could you? Wrote to that Hackney address, but my letter came back. My daughter could have a go at the council. She's a strong character. Told you she tried to punish me, did I? She wrote to Flannery and Mrs Baxter and all the staff, telling them what I should be paying them, telling them I was robbing them blind. Flannery showed me his letter. I was paying him half what my daughter told him he should be getting. So of course, he's never been happy since. I upped his wages a few pounds, but that didn't do. He threatened to leave. Leave, I told him. You leave, Flannery! You're too bloody old to work, anyway. But he never will. He eats practically free. He's got his cottage. He'll die there, or in the spinney poaching pheasants.

Wouldn't do that to your father, would you? Turn his own people against him? Dead is he? Oh. Expect I should be dead, by rights. That dog, Mac, must be dead by now. And those other fleabags, Chuppy and Whatisname. Only thing my wife could pronounce properly in Spanish as far as I know was Narcisco Yepes. Know him? *Narthithco Yepeth!* So how the hell does she manage in Portugoose? Eh? Just wanders about in her sunhat, pointing, I dare say. *Watero las orangerias gracias. Portare immediatementi il breakfastino!* Beats me how you can make a life out of that twaddle! Perhaps she hasn't got a life. She never writes to me. I send her a Christmas card each year, for old time's sake. Sent her an out-of-date printed one last year by mistake: 'With Best Wishes for Christmas and the New Year from Lord and Lady Bressingham', it said! My God, that will have made her break a few ornaments! Fidelity Belcher. I'll wonder to my dying day what happened to her in Macassar.

Show you round the house now. Got a scarf or something? Got any gloves? When I was a boy, there'd be twenty or thirty staying for Christmas. Everybody going in and out of each other's bedrooms in secret! We children used to spy on the night flitters; called them the Somnambulists. Always had a fascination for sex, but Roman Catholics want to take all the fun out of it. Can't imagine why I married one. Didn't suit me at all. I should have had a string of young wives with tearing fingers, like Daff.

Oh, I like your scarf. I like striped things. I told Curry, we're going to build a roller coaster bigger than Battersea! Paint all the structure green, shape the little cars like wasps and bees and let the people yell their heads off, flying above the cedars like insects. Imagine looking out of that window and seeing that – people whizzing over the trees! I'd have loved it. I'd have kept it going round the year. But I expect that's where I went wrong with the council: too keen. Phlegmatic lot! Don't seem to care a jot that Bressingham's sinking into the moat. I told them, give me permission for the funfair and the lion pit and the aviary and I'll put Bressingham on its feet again within a year. I was only asking for *permission*. Not for money. But they refused me. Story of my life: people reaching for their bloody bedjackets and saying, never.

Off we go, then. Always put a macintosh on when I do the tour of the house; protects me from the damp. Dry rot, wet rot, mould, fungus – we've got it all here now. The Somnambulists would turn in their graves! There used to be fires in all the bedrooms and furs on the four-posters. The room Gordon allegedly slept in had a tiger skin as a hearth rug. Can't remember what we did with it. It got the moth, I wouldn't wonder. Or perhaps I sold it off when I bought Lady Bressingham the Quinta San José. I can't remember. Rooms are practically empty, though, now. Don't expect finery, will you? Just a lot of cold, empty rooms now. Nothing much to look at. Terrible legacy, a house like this in an age like this. Glad I haven't got a son to leave it to. Daff's pregnancy was phantom. Did I tell you that? Your gloves match that scarf. Very nice. You're a very bright, lovely woman. If I was younger, you wouldn't be safe with me. Dunno how that phantom got into Daff. Through the air conditioning in the Bentley perhaps! Don't understand women. Never will now, will I? My daughter. Daff. My wife. All potty in one way or another. People are. That's why I wanted to give them a funfair – to let them have a good scream.

A Shooting Season

'You're writing a *what*?'

'A novel.'

Looking away from him, nervously touching her hair, Anna remembered, the last time I saw him my hair wasn't grey.

'Why the hell are you writing a novel?'

Grey hairs had sprouted at forty-one. Now, at forty-five, she sometimes thought, my scalp is exhausted, that's all, like poor soil.

'I've wanted to write a novel ever since I was thirty. Long before, even . . .'

'You never told me.'

'No. Of course not.'

'Why "of course not"?'

'You would have laughed, as you're laughing now.'

Anna had always been enchanted by his laugh. It was a boy's giggle; (you climbed a cold dormitory stairway and heard it bubble and burst behind a drab door!) yet their son didn't have it: at sixteen, he had the laugh of a rowdy man.

'I don't approve.'

'No.'

'It's an act of postponed jealousy.'

Well, if so, then long postponed. Six years since their separation; four since the divorce and his remarriage to Susan, the pert blonde girl who typed his poems. And it wasn't jealousy, surely? In learning to live without him, she had taught herself to forget him utterly. If she heard him talk on the radio, she found herself thinking, his cadences are echoing Dylan Thomas these days; he's remembered how useful it is, if you happen to be a poet, also to be Welsh. Three years older than her, he had come to resemble a Welsh hillside – craggy outcrop of a man, unbuttoned to weather and fortune, hair wiry as gorse. Marcus. Fame clung to his untidy look. No doubt, she thought, he's as unfaithful to Susan as he was to me.

'How did it start?'

The novel-writing, he meant, but he had a way, still, of sending fine ripples through the water of ordinary questions which invited her to admit: I was in love with him for such a long time that parting from him was like a drowning. When I was washed ashore, the sediment of him still clogged me.

'I found there were things I wanted to say.'

'Oh, there always were!'

'Yes, but stronger now. Before I get old and start forgetting.'

'But a *novel?*'

'Why not?'

'You were never ambitious.'

No. Not when she was his: Mrs Marcus Ridley, wife of the poet. Not while she bore his children and made rugs while he wrote and they slept.

'Do your pockets still have bits of sand in them?'

He laughed, took her strong wrist and held her hand to his face. 'I don't know. No one empties them for me.'

*

Anna had been at the rented cottage for three weeks. A sluggish river flowed a few yards from it: mallard and moorhen were the companions of her silence, the light of early morning was silver. In this temporary isolation, she had moved contentedly in her summer sandals, setting up a work table in the sunshine, another indoors by the open fire. Her novel crept to a beginning, then began to flow quietly like the river. She celebrated each day's work with two glasses, sometimes more, of the home-made wine she had remembered to bring with her. She slept well with the window wide open on the Norfolk sky. She dreamed of her book finished and bound. Then one morning Margaret, her partner in her craft business, telephoned. The sound of the telephone ringing was so unfamiliar that it frightened her. She remembered her children left on their own in London; she raced to answer the unforeseen but now obvious emergency. But no, said Margaret, no emergency, only Marcus.

'Marcus?'

'Yes. Drunk and full of his songs. Said he needed to see you.'

'And you told him where I was?'

'Yes. He said if I didn't, he'd pee on the pottery shelf.'

*

'Marcus.'

The rough feel of his face was very familiar; she might have touched it yesterday. She thought suddenly, for all his puerile needs, he's a man of absolute mystery; I never understood him. Yet they had been together for ten years. The Decade of the Poet she called it, wanting to bury him with formality and distance. And yet he surfaced in her: she seldom read a book without wondering, how would Marcus have judged that? And then feeling irritated by the question. On such occasions, she would always remind herself: he doesn't even bother to see the children, let alone me. He's got a new family (Evan 4, Lucy 3) and they, now, take all his love – the little there ever was in him to give.

'You look so healthy, Anna. Healthy and strong. I suppose you always were strong.'

'Big-boned, my mother called it.'

'How is your mother?'

'Dead.'

'You never let me know.'

'No. There was no point.'

'I could have come with you – to the funeral or whatever.'

'Oh, Marcus . . .'

'Funerals are ghastly. I could have helped you through.'

'Why don't you see the children?'

He let her hand drop. He turned to the window, wide open on the now familiar prospect of reed and river. Anna noticed that the faded corduroy jacket he was wearing was stretched tight over his back. He seemed to have outgrown it.

'Marcus . . .?'

He turned back to her, hands in his pockets.

'No accusations. No bloody accusations!'

Oh yes, she noticed, there's the pattern: I ask a question, Marcus says it's inadmissible, I feel guilty and ashamed . . .

'It's a perfectly reasonable question.'

149

'Reasonable? It's a guilt-inducing, jealous, mean-minded question. You know perfectly well why I don't see the children: because I have two newer, younger and infinitely more affectionate children, and these newer, younger and infinitely more affectionate children are bitterly resented by the aforementioned older, infinitely less affectionate children. And because I am a coward.'

He should be hit, she thought, then noticed that she was smiling.

'I brought some of my home-made wine,' she said, 'it's a disgusting looking yellow, but it tastes rather good. Shall we have some?'

'Home-made wine? I thought you were a business*person*. When the hell do you get time to make wine?'

'Oh Marcus, I have plenty of time.'

Anna went to the cold, pament-floored little room she had decided to think of as 'the pantry'. Its shelves were absolutely deserted except for five empty Nescafé jars, a dusty goldfish bowl (the debris of another family's Norfolk summer) and her own bottles of wine. It was thirty-five years since she had lived in a house large enough to have a pantry, but now, in this cupboard of a place, she could summon memories of Hodgson, her grandfather's butler, uncorking Stones ginger beer for her and her brother on timeless summer evenings – the most exquisite moments of all the summer holidays. Then, one summer, she found herself there alone. Hodgson had left. Her brother Charles had been killed at school by a cricket ball.

Anna opened a bottle of wine and took it and two glasses out to her table in the garden, where Marcus had installed himself. He was looking critically at her typewriter and at the unfinished pages of her book lying beside it.

'You don't mean to say you're typing it?'

She put the wine and the glasses on the table. She noticed that the heavy flint she used as a paperweight had been moved.

'Please don't let the pages blow away, Marcus.'

'I'm sure it's a mistake to type thoughts directly onto paper. Writing words by hand is part of the process.'

'Your process.'

'I don't know any writers who type directly.'

'You know me. Please put the stone back, Marcus.'

He replaced the pages he had taken up, put the flint down gently and spread his wide hand over it. He was looking at her face.

'Don't write about me, Anna, will you?'

She poured the wine. The sun touched her neck and she remembered its warmth with pleasure.

'Don't make me the villain.'

'There is no villain.'

She handed him his glass of wine. Out in the sunshine, he looked pale beside her. A miraculous three weeks of fine weather had tanned her face, neck and arms, whereas he . . . how did he spend his days now? She didn't know. He looked as if he'd been locked up. Yet he lived in the country with his new brood. She it was – and their children – who had stayed on in the London flat.

'How's Susan?'

No. She didn't want to ask. Shouldn't have asked. She'd only asked in order to get it over with: to sweep Susan and his domestic life to the back of her mind, so that she could let herself be nice to him, let herself enjoy him.

'Why ask?'

'To get it over with!'

He smiled. She thought she sensed his boyish laughter about to surface.

'Susan's got a lover.'

Oh damn him! Damn Marcus! Feeling hurt, feeling cheated, he thought I'd be easy consolation. No wonder the novel annoys him; he sees the ground shifting under him, sees a time when he's not the adored, successful granite he always thought he was.

'Damn the lover.'

'What?'

He'd looked up at her, startled. What he remembered most vividly about her was her permanence. The splash of bright homespun colour that was Anna: he had only to turn his head, open a door, to find her there. No other wife or mistress had been like her; these had often been absent when he'd searched for them hardest. But Anna: Anna had always *wanted* to be there.

'I'm not very interested in Susan's lover.'

'No. He isn't interesting. He's a chartered surveyor.'

'Ah. Well, reliable probably.'

'D'you think so? Reliable, are they, as a breed? He looks pitiful enough to be it. Perhaps that's what she wants.'

'And you?'

'Me?'

'What do you want, Marcus? Did you come here just to tell me your wife had a lover?'

'Accusations again. All the bloody little peeves!'

'I want to know why you came here.'

'So do I.'

'What?'

'So do I want to know. All I know is that I wanted to see you. If that's not good enough for you, I'll go away.'

Further along the river, she could hear the mallard quacking. Some evenings at sunset, she had walked through the reeds to find them (two pairs, one pair with young) and throw in scraps for them. Standing alone, the willows in front of her in perfect silhouette, she envied the ducks their sociability. No one comes near them, she thought, only me standing still. Yet they have everything – everyone – they need.

'I love it here.'

She had wanted to sit down opposite Marcus with her glass of wine, but he had taken the only chair. She squatted, lifting her face to the sun. She knew he was watching her.

'Do you want me to go away?'

She felt the intermittent river breeze on her face, heard the pages of her novel flap under the stone. She examined his question, knew that it confused her, and set it aside.

'The novel's going to be about Charlie.'

'Charlie?'

'My brother Charles. Who died at school. I'm imagining that he lived on, but not as him, as a girl.'

'Why as a girl?'

'I thought I would understand him better as a girl.'

'Will it work?'

'The novel?'

'Giving Charlie tits.'

'Yes, I think so. It also means she doesn't have to play cricket and risk being killed.'

'I'd forgotten Charlie.'

'You never knew him.'

'I knew him as a boy – through your memories. He of Hodgson's ginger beer larder!'

'Pantry.'

She's got stronger, Marcus decided. She's gone grey and it suits her. And she's still wearing her bright colours. Probably makes not just her own clothes now, but ponchos and smocks and bits of batik to sell in her shops. And of course her son's friends fall in love with her. She's perfect for a boy: bony, maternal and sexy. Probably her son's in love with her too.

'Can I stay for dinner?'

Anna put her glass to her lips and drained it. He always, she thought, made requests sound like offers.

*

Anna scrutinised the contents of the small fridge: milk, butter, a bunch of weary radishes, eggs. Alone, she would have made do with the radishes and an omelette, but Marcus had a lion's appetite. His most potent memory of a poetry-reading fortnight in America was ordering steak for breakfast. He had returned looking ruddy, like the meat.

Anna sighed. The novel had been going well that morning. Charlie, renamed Charlotte, was perched high now above her cloistered schooldays on the windswept catwalk of a new university. Little gusts of middle-class guilt had begun to pick at her well-made clothes and at her heart. She was ready for change.

'Charlotte can wait,' Marcus told Anna, after her one feeble attempt to send him away. 'She'll be there tomorrow and I'll be gone. And anyway, we owe it to each other – one dinner.'

I owe nothing, Anna thought. No one (especially not pretty Susan with her tumbling fair hair and her flirtatious eyes) could have given herself – her time, her energy, her love – more completely to one man than she to Marcus. For ten years he had been the landscape that held her whole existence – one scarlet poppy on the hills and crags of him, sharing his sky.

'One dinner!'

*

She took the car into Wroxham, bought good dark fillet, two bottles of Beaujolais, new potatoes, a salad and cheese.

While she was gone, he sat at the table in the sunshine,

153

getting accustomed to the gently scented taste of her home-made wine and, despite a promise not to, reading her novel. Her writing bored him after a very few pages; he needed her presence, not her thoughts.

I've cried for you, he wanted to tell her. There have been times when – yes, several of them – times when I haven't felt comfortable with the finality of our separation, times when I've thought, there's more yet, I need more. And why couldn't you be part of my life again, on its edge? I would honestly feel troubled less – by Susan's chartered surveyor, by the coming of my forty-ninth birthday – yes, much less, if you were there in your hessian or whatever it is you wear and I could touch you. Because ten years is, after all, a large chunk of our lives, and though I never admit it, I now believe that my best poems were written during those ten and what followed has been mainly repetition. And I wanted to ask you, where are those rugs you made while I worked? Did you chuck them out? Why was the silent making of your rugs so intimately connected to my perfect arrangement of words?

*

'So here we are . . .'

The evening promised to be so warm that Anna had put a cloth on the table outside and laid it for supper. Marcus had helped her prepare the food and now they sat facing the sunset, watching the colour go first from the river, then from the willows and poplars behind it.

'Remember Yugoslavia?'

'Yes, Marcus.'

'Montenegro.'

'Yes.'

'Those blue thistles.'

'Umm.'

'Our picnic suppers!'

'Stale bread.'

'What?'

'The bread in Yugoslavia always tasted stale.'

'We used to make love in a sleeping bag.'

'Yes.'

Anna thought, it will soon be so dark, I won't be able to see him clearly, just as, in my mind, I have only the most indistinct perception of how he *is* in that hard skin, if I ever knew. For a moment she considered going indoors to get a candle, but decided it would be a waste of time; the breeze would blow it out. And the darkness suits us, suits this odd meeting, she thought. In it, we're insubstantial; we're each imagining the other one, that's all.

'I read the novel, as far as you've gone.'

'Yes. I thought you probably would.'

'I never pictured you writing.'

'No. Well, I never pictured you arriving here. Margaret told me you said you "needed" me. What on earth did you mean?'

'I think about you – often.'

'Since Susan found her surveyor?'

'That's not fair.'

'Yes, it's fair. You could have come to see me – and the children – any time you wanted.'

'I wanted . . .'

'What?'

'Not the children. You.'

For a moment, Anna allowed herself to remember: 'You, in the valley of my arms,/ my quaint companion on the mountain./ How wisely did I gather you,/ my crimson bride . . .' Then she took a sip of beaujolais and began:

'I've tried.'

'What?'

'To love other people. Other men, I mean.'

'And?'

'The feelings don't seem to last. Or perhaps I've just been unlucky.'

'Yes. You deserve someone.'

'I don't want anyone, Marcus. This is what I've at last understood. I have the children and the craft shops and one or two men friends to go out with, and now I have the novel . . .'

'I miss you, Anna.'

She rested her chin on folded hands and looked at him. Mighty is a perfect word, she thought. To me, he has always seemed mighty. And when he left me, every room, every place I went to was full of empty space. Only recently had I got used to it, decided finally to stop trying to fill it up. And now there he is again, his enormous shadow, darker, nearer than the darkness.

'You see, I'm not a poet any more.'

155

'Yes, you are, Marcus. I read your new volume . . .'
'No I'm not. I won't write anything more of value.'
'Why?'
'Because I'm floundering, Anna. I don't know what I expect of myself any more, as a poet or as a man. Susan's destroying me.'
'Oh rot! Susan was exactly the woman you dreamed of.'
'And now I have dreams of you.'
Anna sighed and let Marcus hear the sigh. She got up and walked the few yards to the river and watched it shine at her feet. For the first time that day, the breeze made her shiver.

*

Light came early. Anna woke astonished and afraid. Marcus lay on his stomach, head turned away from her, his right arm resting down the length of her body.

A noise had woken her, she knew, yet there was nothing: only the sleeper's breath next to her and the birds tuning up, like a tiny hidden orchestra, for their full-throated day. Then she heard them: two shots, then a third and a fourth. Marcus turned over, opened his eyes and looked at her. She was sitting up and staring blankly at the open window. The thin curtains moved on a sunless morning.

'Anna . . .'
The strong hand on her arm wanted to tug her gently down, but she resisted its pressure, stayed still, chin against her knees.

'Someone's shooting.'
'Come back to sleep.'
'No, I can't. Why would someone be shooting?'
'The whole world's shooting!'
'I must go and see.'
Marcus lay still and watched Anna get up. As she pulled on a faded, familiar gown, both had the same thought: it was always like this, Anna getting up first, Marcus in bed half asleep, yet often watching Anna.

'What are you going to do?'
'I don't know. But I have to see.'
The morning air was chilly. It was sunless, Anna realised, only because the sun had not yet risen. A mist squatted above the river; the landscape was flattened and obscured in dull white. Anna stared. The dawn has extraordinary purpose, she

thought, everything contained, everything shrouded by the light but emerging minute by minute into brightness and shape, so that while I stand still it all changes. She began to walk along the river. The ground under her sandals was damp and the leather soon became slippery. Nothing moved. The familiar breeze had almost died in the darkness, the willow leaves hung limp and wet. Anna stopped, rubbed her eyes.

'Where are you?'

She waited, peering into the mist. The mist was yellowing, sunlight slowly climbing. A dog barked, far off.

'Where are you?'

Senseless question. Where are you? Where are you? Anna walked on. The surface of the water, so near her slippery feet, was absolutely smooth. The sun was climbing fast now and the mist was tumbling, separating, making way for colour and contour. Where *are* you! The three words came echoing down the years. Anna closed her eyes. They came and shot the ducks, she told herself calmly. That's all. Men came with guns and had a duck shoot and the mallard are gone. When I come down here with my scraps, I won't find them. But that's all. The river flows on. Everything else is just as it was yesterday and the day before and the day before that. I am still Anna. Birds don't matter. I have a book to write. And the sun's coming up . . .

She was weeping. Clutching her arms inside the sleeves of the faded gown, she walks from room to room in the empty flat. Where are you! London dawn at the grimed net curtains . . . fruit still in the bowl from which, as he finally went, he stole an orange . . . nothing changes and yet everything . . . his smell still on her body . . . And where am I? Snivelling round the debris of you in all the familiar rooms, touching surfaces you touched, taking an orange from the bowl . . . Where am I? Weeping. The ducks don't matter. Do they? Keeping hold on what is, on what exists *after* the shot has echoed and gone, this is all that's important, yes, keeping hold on what I have forced myself to become, with all the sanding and polishing of my heart's hardness, keeping hold of my life alone that nothing – surely not the wounds of one night's loving? – can destroy. So just let me wipe my face on the same washed-out corner of a sleeve. And forget. A stranger carries the dead mallard home, dead smeared heads, bound together with twine. But the sun comes up on the same stretch of river where, only yesterday, they had life . . .

*

Marcus held Anna. They stood by his car. It was still morning, yet they sensed the tiredness in each other, as if neither had slept at all.

'I'll be going then, old thing. Sorry I was such a miserable bugger. Selfish of me to disturb you with my little problems.'

'Oh, you weren't disturbing me.'

'Yes, I was. Typical of me: Marcus Ridley's Lament for Things as They Are.'

'I don't mind. And last night —'

'Lovely, Anna. Perhaps I'll stop dreaming about you now.'

'Yes.'

He kissed her cheek and got quickly into the car.

'Good luck with the novel.'

'Oh yes. Thank you, Marcus.'

'I'll picture you working by your river.'

'Come and see the children, Marcus. Please come and see the children.'

'Yes. Alright. No promises. Are you going to work on the book today?'

'No, I don't think I can. Not today.'

'Poor Anna. I've tired you. Never mind. There's always tomorrow.'

'Yes, Marcus,' and very gently she reached out and touched his face, 'there's always tomorrow.'

My Love Affair With James I

Exercise 4, Week 4 of the Eric Neasdale 'Make Money by Writing' course: Describe with honesty and, if possible, humour, a recent major event in your life.

William Nichols – or 'Will', as I think of him – is an actor I'd never actually met. It's odd I'd never met him because a) he's filthily famous and b) his pic is on the same page as mine in *Spotlight*. Actually, my pic is above his as I'm fractionally superior to him alphabetwise, but our page goes: Stephen Nias (me), William Nichols (Will), Bob Nickolls (spelt with a k and two l's and pullulating with his resemblance to Alain Delon), and Ken Nightingale (the less said the better; cast as the eternal traffic warden; should never have had his pic in 'Leading').

You may think the question of the *Spotlight* pics is a bit of a waffle (this writing course is tediously keen on the word relevance), but I don't think it is. You see, my pic was actually taken in '79 (hair darker, bags minimal, *you* know . . .) and in it I look so absolutely dead right for the part of the Duke of Buckingham that I was offered it sight unseen, or virtually. I did have lunch with the producer, Alfie Morton, before contracts went out, but Alfie likes to lunch at *The Rasputin*, an utterly excruciating Russian restaurant he thinks is de riguer for the famous, and luckily the bloody Rasputin is so dark – and I mean *pitch* – that you honestly can't tell whether the cav in your blinis is red or black. So you see, in those conditions I could still make thirty-five; Alfie stares at me like an icon over our red-glassed candle and his only worry is, is my voice, which viewers hear almost nightly extolling the nutrient virtues of a catfood called Tiggo, too domesticated a tool for the cadences of the haughty duke? He decides no, and he's right. The reason I got the Tiggo VO is that my voice is – and I say this without vanity – my greatest asset as an actor. I'm not a deep person; I know my failings. Life's a bit of a game to me, a bit of a tap-dance. But my voice is redolent with depth. It's as if it was engendered in one of those *grottes* the green Michelin guides keep encouraging you to visit. It reverbs. It has texture. I'd be dead on for Son et Lumière. I'm wasted on frigging catfood – but that's television for you, and my bank manager isn't complaining. So I have no difficulty convincing Alfie Morton that he and old 'Eyelids' Mordecai, our illustrious director, have made the right choice.

By the time we get to coffee, Alfie's making his 'Welcome Aboard' speech and I know I've got the duke. I actually begin to rattle with excitement: a four-month shoot, one month of which will be in Greece. And Will Nichols playing King James. With Will's name on the picture, it's certainly going to get coverage. It's a major movie alright: Jon Markworthy on script, Billy Nettlefold on cameras, the Morton/Mordecai clout with distributors, Will in his first screen role for over two years, and me. After lunch with Alfie (I put my shades on the minute we get anywhere near natural light) I brisk along to Dougie, my agent, and to my utter amazement he produces a bottle of Taylor's port from a filing cabinet marked 'Clients SS'. I'm much too surprised by the Taylor's gesture to ask Dougie what 'SS' stands for.

When I got home, I took my trousers off and examined my legs. My bathroom's all mirrors, so I shot little glances at them from every angle. They're okay. I'm five eleven. But they're not the exquisite legs the Duke displays in that picture of him in the Portrait Gallery. Those legs look as if they begin at his armpits, and my thighs seem positively neanderthal by comparison. But then I remembered that Will Nichols is a short man – sturdy and stubby – so that compared to his legs, I thought mine would have a touch of the gazelle about them. Heaven knows why I was so worried about legs. There were far more excruciating things to worry about, had I known it at the time (as the lion said to the unicorn), but I was all breezy innocence and excitement! I got out a pair of ancient bermudas and stuffed them out with a couple of cushions to make them look like hose. Protruding from these, my legs looked plain ridiculous.

It's at times like these, with cushions puffing out my bum, that I'm thankful I live alone. At least, after everything that happened, I haven't lost my sense of humour!

*

Reading this, I see that there are two exclamation marks in my last para. The writing course says 'use these sparingly'. May have to cross them out in my rewrite. And the joke about the unicorn: 'Avoid doubtful and distasteful humour' says the bloody course. Never mind. I'll leave it in for now.

*

There was one fact which, from the start of this film, I found slightly odd, but which no one else remarked on: namely, Will Nichols, about to play the most Scottish king since Macbeth, was Welsh. I'd long ago seen Will Nichols grapple with a Scots accent in one of those thunderous war movies that are all about detonating bridges over the Rhine, and he'd done dismally. His voice has what I'd call gusto, but it's unmistakable Welsh gusto. He can do a passable English baronet, but not (well, I don't think he can) a Scots king. I felt like saying to Morton: you might as well cast an American, love, and have done with it. But by the time I was offered Buckingham (the juiciest film part I've ever had) Will Nichols's name was on the project and there it would stick. Over the Taylor's, Dougie told me that at least Will was off the booze.

I'll tell you what I knew about Will at that time. (You'll know most of it already. His life is pretty well public knowledge.) He'd crawled onto a stage bent double from his deprived childhood in a Welsh mine, straightened up enough to do a memorable Hamlet aged twenty, married a then star of the English stage called Myrtle Bridehead, years his senior and opposite whom he played a rather chunky Romeo. (Myrtle Bridehead as Juliet, nudging thirty-seven, was one of the finest embarrassments of my protected youth.) He'd then been whisked off to America. In Hollywood, he began to make a string of romantic movies and by the age of thirty he was a flash name and a millionaire. He should have died then. Or am I being unfair? He's done one or two respectable things since then – he's now forty-seven, looks older – but his fame has bred on itself, rather than on additions to itself, if you get my

161

drift. He dumped Myrtle the minute LA swam into vision through the smog and only played a bit-part at her suicide two months later. Rumour has it that since Myrtle, the last scales of Welsh conformism have fallen from his eyes and that from that time he has tangled off-screen only with men and boys. His most faithful companion of recent years has been the whisky bottle. His Welsh lungs have begun to sound as if they're filling up with coal. Despite all this, he's still a bankable star.

As to me (virtually unknown Steve Nias), I tried to prepare myself meticulously for Buckingham, and I don't just mean staring at my legs. Jon Markworthy's script suggested a relationship between Buckingham and King James which, if it wasn't a love affair in the understood sense, was as least as passionate as one. Now I loathe ambiguity. So I spent hours in Chelsea Public Library trying to decide for myself precisely what the nature of this friendship was – and failing. History itself is ambiguous on the subject, as I might have guessed. So all I had to go on were Markworthy's scenes. In one of these, I am summoned in the middle of the night from the bed of my wife, Katherine, to the bedchamber of the king. I arrive breathless, and no wonder. The king stammers on about his role as 'nurturer of peace in this land'. I, wearing a night robe (that turned out to resemble and to be as heavy as a forty foot drape) start to mutter ominously about the need to take England to war. A verbal scuffle ensues. The King starts to weep. I hold him and he kisses me. *Lorks!* In the run-up to my first meeting with Will Nichols, I phoned Dougie and asked for a meeting with Markworthy and Eyelids re the persistent ambiguity of this and other scenes. Dougie simply laughed and told me to stop jittering.

*

I can't leave *lorks* in. But this one word conveys precisely what I felt every time I read this scene. One of the commandments of the Eric Neasdale Writing Course is 'avoid ejaculations where possible.' *Lorks* is an undoubted ejaculation. Oh well. Perhaps something else will come to me in the middle of the night, as they say. N.B. I must take this piece of work seriously. I would seriously like to become a writer. But writing about 'real events' seems to have its little problems.

*

Before I plunge in to the main thrust of my story (this last is a shitty sentence and must go), I think I ought to say a word or two about my life – as it was before I met Will Nichols, and as it is becoming again.

I came to acting from dancing. The love of dance hasn't entirely left me and I sometimes do little dance routines on the flat roof of my Fulham top-floor flat, among my plants. I grow cucumbers on this roof in the summer and shrubs and herbs and roses all the year round, in big tubs and old baths and sinks. I never grow tomatoes because I'm allergic to them. This allergy makes some dinners problematical: you find tomato in almost everything from *daube* to *douglère*, from Bolognese to braised oxtail, and the unsightly neck rashes I then have to endure are one of the penances of an otherwise quietly agreeable and civilised life.

I live alone, as I said, but I'm seldom actually lonely. I lived with someone called David for a year and with someone called Donovan for about nine months. Otherwise, I've always lived alone since I left school and home. My mother is an elderly person and safely put away in a home for elderly persons near Swindon. My father, who disapproved of me and all my works till his dying day, mercifully reached his dying day in 1976, and since then I've felt guilty about nothing and fairly positive about most things.

The money I make from Tiggo and other VOs I do for ITV have brought me a high standard of living, even though I don't get as much acting work as I'd like. Between you and me, I'm not that fantastic an actor. I've got my following because, as you've guessed from the Buckingham thing, I'm still fairly morbidly handsome. Sexually, I'm what they call alert and I honestly don't have any difficulty in that *département*. My West Indian cleaner, Mrs Baali (I call her Pearl Barley. That's the kind of joke that's typical me) is allowed to tease me about my boyfriends, but I keep them low profile. 'Sex = love' is pure romanticism, pure bunkum, in my view. Jon Markworthy at least understood this in his famous script, if nothing else. I'm a very meticulous person, day to day. I like clean things. Lately, I've been a slut, though. I've had weekends when I didn't wash or shave or go out or wash up. Pearl Barley's been dying to comment. She's like a huge, wobbling brown fruit, my Pearl Barley, and comment on my sluttishness has been on the brink of bursting out of her for several weeks, I can tell. But she hasn't cracked yet. She's a loyal woman. I'm not all that loyal myself, but I value it in others.

Well, that's me. Enough said. On to the main thrust, as they say: my love affair.

I was forty-one the day I met Will Nichols for the first time face to face. An odd coincidence that this project should kick off on my birthday, 6 May. In fact, it had kicked off months before of course, but old Eyelids actually sat down with his lead actors on 6 May in what appeared to be the boardroom of his Wardour Street offices, flanked by Markworthy and Morton and Nettlefold and legions of PAs, and over a rather troppo minceur lunch of smoked salmon mould he began to talk about 'my great new royal baby, King James I'.

'Eyelids' Mordecai is seventy-eight years old. My allergy to tomatoes (uncomfortable enough, God knows) is but a shade compared to the ghostly army of allergies haunting Mordecai. Mordecai rightly belongs in a Swiss sanitorium, muffled to the neck in polyanimide, breathing cloudless air. Here, he would die calmly, snow would settle on his globally famous eyelids and that would be that. As it is, his quaking body is carried on and off aeroplanes, wheeled around scorching Spanish locations in the modern equivalent of a Bath chair. Some days, even his voice has a quake to it and his brain has patches of blank, like sunspots, and all his instructions fall out of his drooling mouth in slow motion, like elephants' feet. It makes you wonder, when you consider what Mordecai earns per annum, about the film business.

The first thing Will told me about Mordecai – on that first day we met, my birthday – was 'don't expect him to direct.' I stared at Will. Our bedroom scenes were still some weeks distant, but prior to them I had been banking on a little 'guidance' from Eyelids. Will then related how, in 1975, Eyelids had cast him as Ulrick Voss in a film he proposed to make of Patrick White's justly famous (but in my view dead difficult) novel, *Voss*. Will invoked his education-deprived childhood to explain his confusion with this man (the casting was moronic, of course. Will Nichols is far too gross a person to play Voss, even in a weightless after-life) and went grovelling to Mordecai for a bit of direction. Mordecai was having one of his quivering and quaking days. They were in southern

Australia in temps of 100° fahrenheit (I can't do this centigrade thing; I'm much too old to learn) and Mordecai's brain was blank white. He told poor old Will to read the book five more times (448pp. in my King Penguin edition and Will had one week), went off to have his morning enema and would not brook the subject again. Luckily – or perhaps in consequence of this sad scene – the film was so excruciatingly bad and so catastrophically over-budget, it was put into turnaround half way through and never re-started. Will caught sunstroke that year and in his fever believed he was getting nearer to understanding the hauntings of Ulrick Voss. Will's life is full of little such ironies.

*

I'm a bit off track, I see. The course says: 'Imagine your subject as a Roman Road (*sic* caps). Its foundation must be your understanding and, except where absolutely necessary, you must try not to veer from it.' I don't know if information about Will and Mordecai is 'absolutely necessary', but I think it might be. (I hate the word 'veer'. There was a boy at school called Vere Pickersgill, whom I loathed.) Pearl Barley's just arrived to do me out. She says all this writing I'm closeted with is making me deadly pale. Better phone Dougie and see if there's a little role-ette for me in a hot clime.

*

I had expected to dislike Will Nichols. The fame and success of other actors can bring on neck rashes as badly as the virulent tomato. And who was Steve Nias compared to Golden Will, the lad from the Rhonda turned superstar? A nothing. An 'SS' in Dougie's vocab. (I'll explain 'SS' later.) But then – and this is the key to the events which followed – who was George Villiers, later Duke of Buckingham, compared to the king himself? A bit of trumped-up gentry with elongated calves. A hitherto also-ran at the court. Until, that is, the king singled him out. Until the king made him his confidant, his favourite, his own Saint John. With his stubborn Scottish hand, King James parted the sea of court bathers and gave Buckingham the Navy. Henceforth he was dressed, metaphorically anyway, in sapphires.

At the end of that first afternoon in Mordecai's boardroom,

just as I was about to sally home to water my cucumbers, Welsh Will invited me to tea. Mumbling something about needing to get to know each other better 'before the schedules start to bite', he shepherded me into his chauffeur-driven Jag and I was whisked off to Claridge's. (Will is a tax exile now and has no home in England other than Claridge's, which he treats exactly as if he owned it all.)

In his sumptuous suite, decorated in remarkably subtle shades of pale lemon and oyster grey, he ordered iced tea (a Californian fad I utterly loathe; it reminds me of my two years at Ipswich rep), then sent his secretary and other minions away and began to talk. He talked about exile. My eye wandered to an Indian rug which totally complemented the shades of the room, adding blue and a hint of white. I sort of waded in the lovely symmetries of the rug's pattern while Will's coal-silted voice rasped on about the loneliness of LA and Monaco. I was dying to ask Will where he'd found the rug (grey and yellow with blue and white are dead unusual colours in Indian wool work) but he was embarked on a monologue and I couldn't get my question in.

Gradually, over the field of the rug, Will's talking began to hang like a nearing thunderstorm. I stared up at him, sensing in his gaelic heart gigantic rain clouds. And lo, over the cragged hillsides of his cheeks, rivulets of tears began to beat down! I felt *livid*. Honestly, I did. Used. Acted upon in more ways than one. 'God,' I felt like saying, 'if you understood the sacrifices us lesser mortals have to make for our so-called art (and the frigging Tiggo VOs aren't the only ones) you wouldn't be blubbing about fame's adverbial negatives and qualifying clauses. You'd be admiring the management's superlative flower arrangements and saying to yourself, fortunate me! Life had me marked out for rickets and TB and all I got was success.'

But I'm a soft-hearted person. I poured Will a brandy and said: 'I'm terribly relieved you're such a sensitive thing, Will. James I was a terribly sensitive man. And you know what he said about privilege? "The taller be the trees, the harder doth the wind blow on them." '

Then I left. It was a hot day and my bloody birthday and I wasn't going to waste it all on Will.

We were shooting the interiors at Pinewood. Designer,

Geoff Hamm, had done a great job on the Theobalds sets and on Day One old Eyelids' pearly veins were rippling with expectation. Dougie's assistant, an intelligent, pretty person called Victoria, had sent flowers to my dressing room. I'd never had the flower treatment before and they put me in a lovely mood. Jon Markworthy, reputedly sulking in his tent like Achilles over script changes commanded by Eyelids, turned out not to be sulking at all and had done a nice new scene between me and Jimmie Henraes, the very dear actor playing Charles (later Charles I), the King's son. So all seemed set fair. I was feeling just the right amount of mingled fear and excitement. Makeup did a super job on my bags and this and my black wig took five years off me, or more. Ready, steady, go, I thought. But then Will appeared. Eyes like fried eggs, capilliaries popping like a coral forest, tongue like old pipes. Terror and self-pity had led him back to demon drink, the whole process begun, I later learned, by the single brandy I had poured him at the Claridge.

Mordecai's voice grew guttural with suppressed rage. Will threw up into one of Geoff Hamm's supposedly Jacobean fireplaces and was laid to rest in his dressing room with Vichy water and Aludrox. The entire first day's schedule was changed and I spent the day mainly unused, just feeling ancient inside my wig.

Will slept through most of the day, then woke up and ordered a bottle of claret, which was evidently brought him because at five, when he asked to see me, he'd already drunk half of it and was looking better.

He apologised to me. At least he had the grace to do this. He also apologised for crying in Claridge's. Then he said, quite utterly out of the blue: 'there's only two who are going to funk it on this picture, Steve, and that's you and me.'

I poured myself a glass of his Château Something and sat myself down in his idiotic rocking chair. (Will Nichols has this sentimental stick of furniture flown and carted to every dressing room and every caravan he's ever worked from. It's his 'trademark'. You could have gone on a world cruise with the travelling money that rocking chair has consumed.) I said something reasonably lame about not intending to 'funk it', but he cut me off. 'I,' he said majestorily, 'shall fail because I no longer have the courage or the voice a talent like mine requires, and you, Steve, will fail because this part has come to you ten years too late.'

*

I don't know, but I think I'm in my stride a bit now. I think my writing's got a bit better as this story's gone on. That's because I'm worrying less about Neasdale's rules and just trying to remember what happened and put it down. There are still words I'll have to alter, though, like 'frigging'. Dougie phoned. The VO Clinic (as I call it) want me to do Buffi-pads nappy liners. Have I reached my nadir, prostitutionwise?

*

For as long as we were in England, I was able to steer clear of Will, except actually on set. The schedule (and the script) were redrafted to enable Will to 'get into' King James rather better than he appeared to be doing before the big key emotional scenes were asked of him. In Mordecai's age-yellowed eyes, you could visibly see thoughts about replacing him doing battle with dollar signs. Cut his losses now and re-start the movie in a year's time with a new star? Keep Will on, stay more or less inside budget, take the risk he'd pull something out in the big scenes? Some mornings Eyelids would look used up, poor old thing, as if he'd died in the night, but then out would come some quavery instruction and the hopeless day would start.

Will was dead right about him not directing. I came to rely on Markworthy (and thank God he was around) to help me step by step through Buckingham. Markworthy is a very plain (I don't mean ugly) and honest and kind man – a far cry indeed from the petulant Marxists masquerading as dramaturges I've had the misfortune to meet at play rehearsals in condemned warehouses. Markworthy seems to handle success as if it were Health Food. It's made him extremely calm and sensible and you sense that his bowel movements are exquisite. I rather envy him. And we've stayed in touch. He and his wife, Jane, grow cucumbers in Barnes (a great bond, the growing of things) and I've entertained them on my rooftop.

But on. Markworthy didn't come with us to Greece. (Let me just mention that the bit of the film we were to make in Greece was, in the script, meant to be made in Spain. Now, in most filmscripts, if the writer has been foolish enough to suggest Africa, India, Australia, Ceylon, Mexico, or anywhere parched-seeming, these bits are invariably made in Spain. In our case, we had a bonafide reason for shooting in Spain – namely that Buckingham and Prince Charles did actually go to Spain to woo the Infanta Donna Maria and are visited there (in the film, but *not* in the history books) by the king. But such is the pachydermic stupidity of this business that we lugged ourselves and our hardware an extra thousand miles, to dress one country up as another far closer to home. Perhaps we were getting money from the Greek Film Foundation, or whatever. I honestly have no idea. I didn't even feel it was worth mentioning to Dougie, let alone to Alfie or Eyelids. Play the part, Nias, and shut up.)

*

I'm having a lot of trouble with my brackets. The problem is, quite a portion of my life seems to lie within this particular form of punctuation. Neasdale doesn't seem to have a rule here.

*

So, no, Jon Markworthy couldn't come with us to Greece, which was a blow for me. He was off on a talking tour of seventeen American cities, and we were flown to an arrid bit of Olympian hinterland we immediately christened Poxos. Poxos had one verdant edge – palms and cypress and yuccas and hibiscus and the sound of a bird or two, and hidden in the verdure a sublimely beautiful seventeenth-century palazzo, undergoing conversion to a 5-star hotel. It was called the Palladium Hotel, which gave rise to a series of panto gags among our irreverent group, brought on not merely by the name, but also by the fact that we weren't actually *staying* at the Palladium; the Palladium was our location – the King of Spain's alleged summer palace, the setting for our scenes with the infanta. (According to history, all these scenes took place in Madrid itself. Someone suggested Eyelids would pass on if forced to consume the oily paellas of that city.)

We were billeted – and this included our star, Will and his rocking chair – in a modern motel called the Eleusis, upon whose low-fashioned concrete walls the summer *meltimi* wind remorselessly blew, from six in the morning till dusk. At dusk, having boiled your mind to leaden grey meat all day, it died. You began to hear the birds and the crickets. You relaxed. The terrace of your favourite taverna would be bathed in last light. You began to drink.

Jimmie Henraes drank to forget Mary Powell (the actress playing Katherine, who wasn't in the Spanisho-Greek sequences) and with whom he had fallen in love that day in Eyelids' boardroom. (A love consummated so many times during the Pinewood days, poor old Jimmie could hardly stagger through a scene without having a lie-down.) Morton and Mordecai drank with some rotund Greek businessmen who had appeared in suits on Day One. Nettlefold and the crew drank Greek beer and spent a lot of time scorching the sparse local flora with untreated urine. Geoff Hamm developed piles and drank in solitary pain. And I, well I drank because I was there and because, by that time, I had fallen under the spell of Will Nichols.

I was so balanced, I thought. I knew what Will Nichols was – a failed genius, a lush, an egomaniac. But what he still had, and this I suppose was why he was still a star, was a terrible and irresistible charm. I say terrible because honestly I thought at forty-one I was immune to anything so *peripheral* as charm. I'm a wicked flirt, but I'm jolly hard to ensnare. I actually think my ensnarement stemmed from what Will had said about the two of us funking our roles. I'd become determined to prove him wrong – not only as far as I was concerned, but also as far as *he* was concerned. Can you understand this? I wanted to be a marvellous Buckingham, but I knew I could only do this if I helped Will (yes, *helped* him) to be a marvellous King James. And he sensed this in me. He sensed, right after the tea in Claridge's, that I wanted to help him, to nanny him, to love him through it, if you like. And don't forget, he was a lonely, exiled man, terrified out of his skull. He knew he'd get sweet nothing from Mordecai. He didn't get on with Jon Markworthy, as I did. So he plonked himself on me. James's obsessive need of Buckingham somehow became utterly mixed and mingled with Will's need of me. Will's psyche was just as plagued by imaginary enemies as the king's. He saw enemies all around him. He had dreams of terrible persecutions and woundings. He needed a shrink, I suppose, and instead he found a soft heart – yours truly, Steve.

*

Pearly Barley has an amazing son, who calls himself T-Bone Jack. He wants to be a rock star, she says with a groan. He just arrived to collect her in a borrowed Cortina. Pearl B. insisted on showing him my roof garden, so I went up with them. T-Bone Jack has the hardest eyes and the tightest buttocks I've ever seen on any man, ethnic or no. Yet, surprisingly, his handshake was rather soft and moist. N.B. Must remember to expunge all random jottings (i.e. about T-Bone's buttocks) when I commit this piece to my stone-age Olympia portable.

*

On the fifth day at Poxos, we reached one of our key scenes. Finding Buckingham's absence from England unbearable, King James has crossed the treacherous water and arrives in Spain. Paying scant respect to the King of Spain (an excellent Mexican actor, Leoncio Iagos – known of course to us as 'Iago') or to the infanta (an American actress, Jane Bellamy, doing ineffectual battle with Spanish consonants), he strides in to Buckingham's lavish suite of rooms and tells him he 'cares not a jot for England, nor for any man on this earth' if he is to be deprived of his 'Sweet Steenie's presence'. ('Steenie', as you probably know, was James's pet name for George Villiers, Duke of Buckingham, derived from the angelic St Stephen. The fact that my name is Steve seems to have been, in Will Nichols's confused subconscious, additional vindication of his need of me.) An exceedingly emotional duet is then played out: Steenie refuses to return to England until he's nabbed the infanta for Prince Charles; James says he will die if he returns alone. Cut, meanwhile, to a posse of wily Spaniards, who start to mumble into their ruffs in the following vein: 'Willst you not remark, my dear assembled lords, that James of England hath, by his untimely passage, vouchsafed to us a timely royal hostage?' (This entire scene is historical bunkum. As I have previously noted, I learned in Chelsea Library that James never went to Spain. However, it thickens the plot nicely and gives to Will and me another challenging scene.)

I was dreading these scenes. I'd begun to have dreams of

London and soothing wet weather. The *meltimi* and the retsina and Will's talk of his infancy and the dust of Poxos were starting to get up my nostrils. I still wanted to help Will, but fear of my big scenes with him weren't allayed by his ongoing drink situation (as I heard Alfie Morton describe Will's attachment to the flagellating local wine).

But then Will pulls it off, as they say. On the first take, there he is, line-perfect, his Welsh-cum-Scottish voice at last singing with absolutely convincing pain, his hands pawing me in perfectly convincing Jamesian little futile gestures, his eyes starting to brim with the jewel in the brave actor's crown – on-camera tears. The floor is hushed. Mordecai signals to Nettlefold to keep turning over. And as Will at last pulls me to him and breaks down, sobbing out his months of loneliness and fear, I feel my heart start to pound with the thrill, the utter euphoria of being in the arms of a great actor.

Well, I'm not that young, as I've told you (my bags were brutal that day, what with the wind and the early starts), but I am a very over-sensitive man. There's a lot of the child in me. I've never quite got over my love of excitement and fame. And although you'll be thinking I should have known better at my age, I can only tell you that then and there, in the fly-blown Palladium, with a battery of 2Ks masquerading as sunlight and Eyelids Mordecai staring at me like an anorexic iguana, in the mingled smells of the Robin starch on Will's ruff and his Pour la Vie aftershave on his bearded neck, I was caught with my rib cage down and my unprotected heart fell suddenly and hopelessly in love.

I went back to Wardrobe quaking and shaking from the triumph of our scene. It's all turned, I thought. From now on, the film will start to work. In fact it will be a good movie. And the high spots will be my scenes with Will. I longed for the rest of these scenes now. Playing opposite Will, I knew I could be superb. There might even be a 'Best Supporting' Oscar in it, or at least a BAFTA nomination, who could say? I took off my costume with trembling hands, felt my lips quiver as my wig was hung on its friendly buff wigstand. So, out into the night, I thought! Have a shower, then on with the white seersucker blouson and down to the taverna to start the hot night's revels with Will!

Well, I sat in the taverna for two hours. I toyed with the

goatsmeat kebabs, swished down a couple of carafes of red. Jimmie Henraes came and sat with me and we talked about England and Mary Powell. The *meltimi* dropped and the lovely evening quiet came on. At the next table, Nettlefold and some of the crew were talking excitedly (for a camera squad) about the day. But Will didn't show. At ten thirty, I went back to the Eleusis. Will was in his room, but his light was out. Someone said he'd gone to bed straight after we'd finished shooting. I went to my room and tried to sleep. I tried to stop it, but under the thin covers, I knew my whole body was shaking.

*

One of the instructions in the Eric Neasdale Writing Course is 'Always write about what you know. Unless you actually are a blind philatelist, do not try to write about this.' Well I disagree on two counts with this instruction. Firstly, I think, if you're going to bother to be a writer, which isn't exactly a laugh-a-minute kind of life, you might as well also bother to see how far your putrid imagination can travel – even (sorry, E.N.) into blindness or philately or both, because why not? Secondly, the question of what one *knows* is much more complex than what is suggested here. I think so, anyway. For instance, do I, through my recent experience, actually *know* a jot more about the following: James I, George Villiers, Will Nichols, the psyche of actors, the price of success, seventeenth-century English civilisation, twentieth-century Greek civilisation, love, infatuation, envy, childhood, Welsh miners and so on? I'm not sure. But all these are vital ingredients in the *knowing* of something I can only fully understand by writing about it. (This last sentence is very confused. I know what I mean, however!)

*

Will had complained, since arriving in Greece, that his Mogadon had stopped working and that sleep was a fiasco, hardly worth bothering with. On previous nights, he'd kept me up till two or three, talking and talking, yet on this night – when I felt we at last had something to say to each other – he'd gone to sleep at eight and stuck his ne déranger svp sign on his door. I felt, and I admit this is childish, cheated. I mean, willingly that night would I have stayed carousing with Will. I can be terribly charming when I want and I felt pretty sure of my terrain that extraordinary evening. Instead, I went miserably to bed and shivered and shook till I heard the bloody wind get up, and in the mournfulness of the *meltimi* cried myself to brief sleep.

Because by then I'd understood. It's not complex. I'd read all the signs right and a more intelligent man than me would have understood right away, but it took me most of the night. In the run up to his first big scene (with me, as it happened, but this is neither here nor there) Will had used me, as I've already explained, to help him conquer fear. And today? When the first big scene was safely over? Well, quite simply, I'd done too good a job. I'd played nurse to Will's terror for five weeks and, through me, he had managed to stumble through self-loathing, alcoholic fog and sheer funk out into a mood reminiscent of his younger self, when he was sober, energetic, imaginative and as an actor extremely fine. Today, as he'd held me against his hot, tear-stained face, he knew he'd done it. The king is himself again! Let the resurrection of Will Nichols begin! Really, it's terribly simple. I'm just the ninny who didn't see what was happening till it was too late. ('Write about what you *know*', says Neasdale. If only I'd *known* what Will was doing to me!)

I expect I sound dreadfully self-pitying, don't I? I mustn't whinge, because life goes on, as they say, and actually, now that I'm getting over all my feelings about Will and settling back into what I call 'my little Fulham routine' – my plants, the odd dance to Berlioz on the roof, civilised meals with old friends, visits to the NT and the Barbican (Jimmie Henraes, who married Mary Powell, is currently doing a lovely Benedick in *Much Ado*) and of course sessions at the VO Clinic to pay the housekeeping etc – now that I'm becoming myself again (I've decided I *will* do Buffi-pads), I can at least laugh about my own gullibility, and I know this is a sign there's been no permanent damage.

The bloody old film, now entitled *The Wisest Fool*, comes out next spring and there's rumour of a Royal Gala Performance. If forced to go (and Dougie will force me, because I'm one of his 'SS' clients, the *senza soldi* boys, the ones who haven't quite got there and who need to be 'seen' therefore), I think I'll dress my Pearl Barley up in quivering sequins and take her along on my arm. She, at least, will know where to stick such a piece of artifice.

ABOUT THE AUTHOR

In 1983 Rose Tremain became a Fellow of the Royal Society of Literature. In that same year, she was one of twenty young writers chosen to represent the Best of Young British Novelists in a major promotional campaign. Ms. Tremain has written three novels—*Sadler's Birthday, Letter to Sister Benedicta,* and *The Cupboard.* She is married and lives in Norwich, England.